365 Fairy Tales

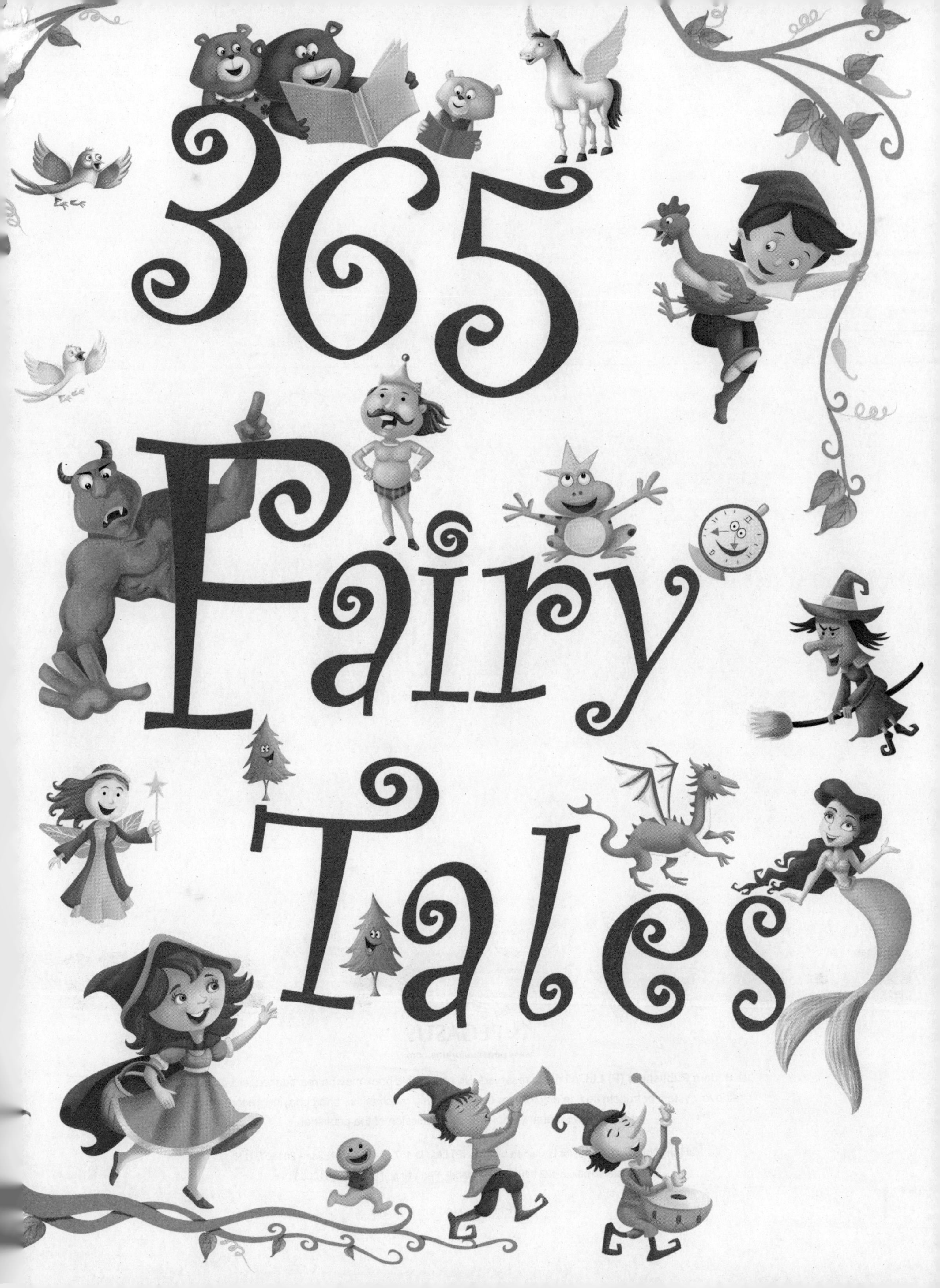

PEGASUS
www.pegasusforkids.com

Published by Kuldeep Jain for B. Jain Publishers (P) Ltd., D-157, Sector 63, Noida - 201307, U.P
Registered office: 1921/10, Chuna Mandi, Paharganj, New Delhi-110055

Printed in India

CONTENTS

JANUARY

FEBRUARY

MARCH

APRIL

MAY

JUNE

JULY

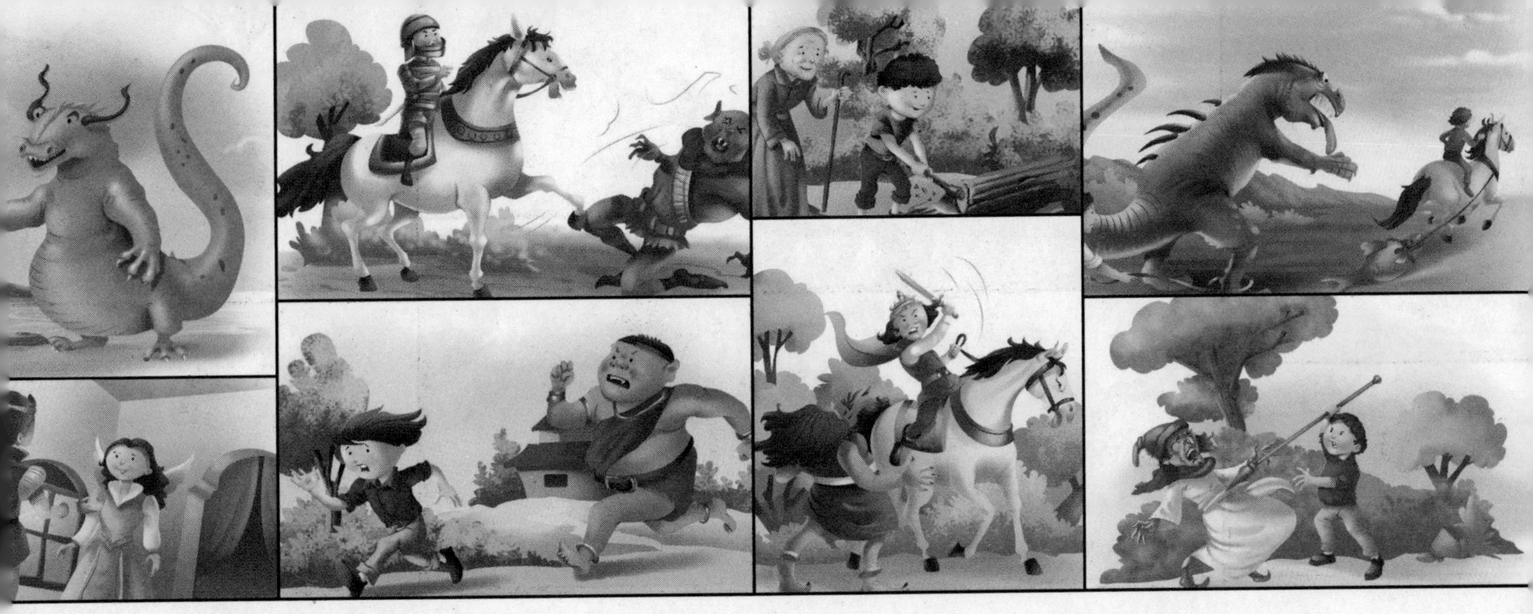

AUGUST

SEPTEMBER

OCTOBER

NOVEMBER

DECEMBER

JANUARY 1

Cinderella

Cinderella had a wicked stepmother and stepsisters who made her work always. Once, they all went to a ball in the palace, leaving Cinderella behind. Cinderella was sad until her Fairy Godmother appeared and waved her wand. Cinderella turned into a beautiful princess with glass slippers. But Fairy Godmother warned, 'Be back before the clock strikes twelve.'

The prince fell in love with Cinderella and danced with her at the ball. The clock struck twelve and Cinderella rushed out, leaving one of her slippers behind. The prince went to every house in his kingdom with the slipper until he found Cinderella. Soon, they were happily married.

JANUARY 2

Petunia and Dahlia

Long ago, an old woman lived with her two daughters, Petunia and Dahlia.

Once, a wicked witch carried Petunia to her castle.

When Dahlia grew older, she set-off into a thick forest at the end of which stood the witch's castle.

On her way to the witch's castle, Dahlia saved a hare's family from a hunter. The Mother Hare thanked Dahlia and said, 'The witch hides her life in her magic wand.'

When Dahlia reached the castle, the witch was sleeping. Dahlia threw the magic wand into the fire and the witch died at once. She then rescued Petunia from the dungeons and they ran home to their mother.

JANUARY 3

The Fairies and the Unicorn Ponies

Once, two fairies of Fairyland were punished by the Fairy Godmother for being naughty. She said, 'You will take care of the Unicorn ponies till their parents return at night.'

The moment, the Unicorn parents left the house, the fairies started arguing about babysitting. They did not notice that the two Unicorn ponies were running out of the house.

Soon, the fairies realised their mistake and frantically looked everywhere for the ponies. They decided to follow the footprints of the ponies and finally found them. They fed the ponies and put them to bed.

The Fairy Godmother rewarded the fairies for their hard work.

JANUARY 4

The Magic Carpet

Long ago, there lived an old witch who weaved carpets. Her little grandson Alex lived with her.

Alex's friends rode bicycles to school. They mocked him for not having one.

One day, Alex angrily said, 'I can always ride on my grandmother's magic carpet.'

When the old witch heard about this, she said, 'Alex, why did you say such a thing? I use my powers only for good. I will weave a magic carpet but promise me that you will not tell anyone.'

Alex promised. He rode on the magic carpet at nights and never told anyone about it.

JANUARY 5

The Woodcutter and the Fairy

Once, a poor woodcutter found a wounded crane in the forest. He took her home and nursed her back to life.

She turned into a fairy and said, 'I am in love with your kindness. I want to be your wife.'

Thus, they were married.

The fairy said, 'I will make beautiful pots and you can sell them in the market. But promise that you will never enter the room where I make pots.'

The woodcutter agreed and grew rich soon.

But the curious woodcutter peeped inside the room, one day. As he broke his promise, the fairy flew away.

JANUARY 6

The Fairy Princess

Once, a king and his son were travelling through a forest. While they were camping in the night, the prince saw a beautiful woman hiding behind a tree.

She said, 'I am the fairy princess. I come from a land where there is no pain or fear. You can come and be the prince there.'

The king angrily asked the fairy to go away. Before she left, she threw a magical apple from her land at the prince.

The prince fell in love with the fairy. So, when he ate the apple, he magically turned into a fairy and disappeared.

JANUARY 7

The Ogre and his Seven Daughters

Once, there was a poor shepherd named Danny. Tired of being poor, Danny thought, 'I have to slay the ogre who lives in the forest. The king has announced hundred gold coins to anyone who kills him. Besides, I can keep the precious crowns of the ogre's daughters.'

On his way, a kind witch gave him a magical sword. Danny killed the ogre with it.

The ogre's daughters were actually fairies who were imprisoned by him. They happily gave their crowns to Danny. He was also rewarded by the king with hundred gold coins.

Danny was never poor again.

JANUARY 8

Rumpelstiltskin

Once, a miller lied to the king that his daughter could spin straw into gold. The king locked the girl, ordering to spin a roomful of straw into gold Shocked, the girl started crying..

Suddenly, a goblin appeared, saying, 'If you give me your first child, I will spin the straw into gold.' The girl agreed. The goblin spun straw into gold.

The happy king married the girl.

Soon, the queen had a child. Days later, the goblin arrived before the queen. She pleaded the goblin to spare her child. He said, 'Only if you guess my name in three days!'

The queen's guesses were all wrong. On the third night, she answered, 'Rumpelstiltskin!'

The goblin angrily disappeared and never returned.

JANUARY 9

Red Riding Hood

Once, a girl called Red Riding Hood walked through a forest with a basketful of food for her sick grandmother. Just then, a wolf appeared and asked, 'Where are you going?'

Red Riding told him about her grandmother. The wicked wolf ran to grandmother's house before her. He went inside pretending to be Red Riding and locked grandmother in a cupboard.

Then, he disguised as grandmother waited for Red Riding. Just as she entered, he pounced on her.

But a woodcutter heard her cries and killed the wolf. Then, they feasted on the food brought by Red Riding Hood.

JANUARY 10

The Farmer's Sweet Potatoes

Once, there lived a farmer who grew sweet potatoes on his farm. But no matter what he did, his sweet potatoes were not sweet enough.

One day, his wife said, 'Why don't you pray to the nature fairies? They will surely help you.'

The farmer prayed to the nature fairies as his wife suggested. The nature fairies were more than happy to help him. They waved their magic wands and the sweet potato plants started shining.

After a week, when the farmer tasted the sweet potatoes, they were delicious. The farmer thanked the nature fairies and earned a huge profit by selling his sweet potatoes.

JANUARY 11

The Elves and the Vegetables

Long ago, there lived a man named Albert who owned a vegetable shop. He took great care of the vegetables.

One day, Albert had to go on a business trip and told his son, 'Take good care of the vegetables.'

The son did not know that little elves always helped kind Albert in his shop.

But, he was lazy and careless in his work. So, the elves magically made all the vegetables disappear to teach him a lesson.

The frightened son apologised to Albert when he returned. Albert spoke to the elves and they returned the vegetables back.

JANUARY 12

The Fairy Princess' Birthday Party

Once, a proud fairy princess invited all the magical creatures to her birthday party.

The entire fairyland came bearing many gifts for her.

The elves brought wonderful toys, the dwarves brought precious diamonds and the goblins brought a magical sword.

The witches gifted her medicinal herbs, the mermaids brought a beautiful conch and the unicorns brought moonbeams.

But the proud fairy princess did not like any of them.

Then, the sprite prince brought a big basket of apples. He said, 'Accept this humble gift from me.'

The fairy princess felt embarrassed for being proud and thanked everyone for their gifts.

JANUARY 13

The Dwarf Family

Once, a family of dwarves lived deep inside a forest. Father dwarf was a diamond miner and wanted his three sons to take up mining for their living.

But the three young dwarves hated their father's job.

Father dwarf asked, 'Then what do you want to do?'

The first son said, 'I want to be a tailor.' The second son said, 'I want to be a baker.' The third son said, 'I want to be a fortune-teller.'

Father dwarf loved his sons a lot so he gave them permission to follow their dreams. The three dwarves became very successful.

JANUARY 14

A Delightful Trick

Once, there lived a beautiful elf princess named Serena.

The elf king had announced, 'As elves are supposed to be the most mischievous creatures of the magical world, I would like to marry Serena to an elf who plays a delightful trick on a human.'

So, all the elves set out after sunset to work on their tricks. Some stole calves from cattle, some stole milk and others jewels.

An elf named Adam gave eyesight to a blind man and vanished. The man was delighted with his eyesight.

Adam won the contest!

He married Serena and lived happily ever after.

JANUARY 15

Jake and the Leprechaun

Long ago, Jake strayed away while helping his father gather wood in the forest.

Just then, a small man dressed in a red coat with brown pants and a green pointed hat appeared before him.

He said, 'Hello Jake, I am a leprechaun. Would you like to see our little leprechaun village?' When Jake agreed, the leprechaun showed him many tiny houses made in the bark of trees.

As Jake was led to the outskirts of the forest, the leprechaun said, 'Alas, we will soon die if more trees are cut!'

Thereafter, Jake encouraged everyone to stop cutting trees.

JANUARY 16

The Kind Hobgoblins

Once, an orphan girl, Carrie was raised by her cruel aunt.

She had to go to the forest stream to bring water every day. There, she sang sad songs about her life.

One morning, Carrie was surprised to see the house cleaned, the clothes washed and food ready.

That night, Carrie hid in the kitchen and saw hobgoblins doing the chores.

When Carrie came out, the hobgoblins said, 'We heard your sad songs and felt sorry for you. So, we have come to help you.'

From then on, Carrie started keeping cheese for the kind hobgoblins as a token of love.

JANUARY 17

The Tail Feathers of a Peacock

Once, the fairy queen sent a giant to guard a nymph as an evil wizard wanted to capture her.

The giant had hundred eyes placed all over his body. He never closed all his eyes at once.

The wizard knew that a melodious song could put all the giant's eyes to sleep and he did just that. But before he could take the Nymph away, the giant woke up and saved her.

The angry wizard killed the giant and escaped.

The sad fairy queen placed the giant's eyes on the tail feathers of a Peacock, in return for his service.

JANUARY 18

The Small Brown Man

One summer, little Matthew went to visit his grandparents in the countryside. While looking for a book in the attic, he saw a small brown man standing behind an old cupboard.

Before Matthew could say something, he disappeared.

Matthew's grandfather chuckled, 'Oh, you must have seen a Brownie. He is a helpful household creature. He has lived in the attic for a long time.'

His grandmother added, 'He disappears if seen by anyone. To befriend him, just leave some bread and cream by the old cupboard.'

Matthew did as he was told and thus befriended a good friend for life.

JANUARY 19

The Magical Bird

Once, a king was troubled by strange events in his kingdom. His minister said, 'Your Majesty, many men have vanished either deep in mines, over cliffs, or into rivers and seas. It usually starts when they see a beautiful bird with shiny feathers.'

When the king went to find the magical bird, he met a tree Nymph, who said, 'The magical bird cannot fly because it eats only gold and silver. Hence its feathers shine.'

The king thanked the nymph and went to search the flightless bird. When he found the bird, he locked it in a cave, thus saving his kingdom.

JANUARY 20

The Prince and the Mermaids

Long ago, a prince was sailing back to his country. The prince saw that his men were tired and hungry. Then, suddenly, he saw an island with many trees and plants.

The prince screamed, 'Head towards the island.!'

As the ship approached the island, the men smelt a sweet fragrance. Suddenly, the prince saw a group of mermaids signalling them from the water. One of them shouted, 'Don't go there. It is a large sea monster's back. You are mistaking him for an island.'

Just then, the sea monster rose but the ship escaped the monster. The prince thanked the mermaids and headed home.

JANUARY 21

The Mountain Fairies

Once, an Old Woman took Lily her sick grandchild to many doctors in her village. But they could not heal the ailing child.

Then, a wise man suggested, 'Why don't you go to the mountains and meet the Old Witch there?'

When the Old Woman met the Witch, she said, 'I will help Lily only if you let her stay here. The mountain air will keep her healthy.'

The poor Woman agreed.

Then the Witch prayed to the Mountain Fairies who had the abilities to heal the sick. Lily was healed very soon and she stayed with Witch in the mountains.

JANUARY 22

The Magical Horses

Long ago, a King was gifted with two magical horses by his fairy godmother for his noble work. The horses had a gift of foretelling future.

The horses started loving their master dearly. So loyal were they that they warned him of any natural disaster or war. They even shared secrets of the fairyland.

Thus, the king became proud and forgot his duties.

The fairy godmother was upset with the horses for sharing magical secrets. So, she took away the horses' gift of speech and separated them from their beloved master.

Thus, the king was also punished for his pride.

JANUARY 23

The Mermaid's Girdle

Long ago, Wayne was fishing alone in the sea. As a storm was approaching, he decided to throw his net one last time. When the net came out, he found a girdle.

That night, Wayne heard a melodious song in his dream. The next day, he saw a lovely mermaid sitting on a rock.

The mermaid said, 'Wayne, I believe you have my girdle. It is said that the mermaid who owns it must grant any wish the man wants.'

Wayne wished for a huge fishing ship and his wish was granted.

He returned the girdle and thanked the mermaid.

JANUARY 24

The Blue Veiled Fairy

Long, long ago, the Blue Veiled Fairy, who protects wild animals, rivers and streams, was once called to a fairy gathering.

The fairy godmother said, 'Blue Veiled fairy, I am assigning jobs to all fairies. I want you to take up the important responsibility of bringing 'Winter'.'

The Blue Veiled Fairy said, 'But why me?' The fairy godmother said, 'I chose you because you are sincere and prompt.'

The Blue Veiled Fairy agreed and she was given a staff that froze whatever it touched during the 'Winter' months. This is how we get winter! The Blue Veiled Fairy brings it!

JANUARY 25

The Witch and the Magical Bird

Long ago, a knight was hunting in a forest. While aiming at a deer, he accidentally stepped on a snake and was bitten.

The knight somehow managed to walk to a cottage at the end of the forest.

An old witch lived in the cottage. When she saw the knight, she felt sorry for him. She uttered a spell:

'Come, come!

O Magical Bird with pure white feathers.

Come, heal this man if you desire.'

A large bird flew from the sky, sucked the poison and spat it out.

The knight thanked the witch and the bird for saving him.

JANUARY 26

Ella and the Wood Fairies

Princess Ella loved to read about fairies.

One day, Ella was having a picnic with her parents in the woods. She wandered away hoping to see fairies.

The wood fairies came to know about Ella's love for the fairies. So, they decided to befriend Ella.

Ella saw a large butterfly sit on her hand. Two tiny girls were riding on the butterfly. The wood fairies said, 'We came to meet you as you longed to see us, Ella.'

Ella was overjoyed and played with them all day. Thereafter, she always went to the woods to play with the wood fairies.

JANUARY 27

The Mermaid and the Prince

Once, a prince fell in love with a mermaid. He wanted to marry her. She said, 'Mermaids become mortals if they marry humans. But we must always stay away from the sea.'

The prince promised to keep her away from the sea. So, the mermaid married the prince.

Then, one day, the queen took the mermaid to a sea shore. The call of the sea was so loud that the mermaid tried to go to the sea. Suddenly, the prince came on his horse and carried her away.

They lived happily ever after and never went near the sea again!

JANUARY 28

The Worthy Ruler

Once, a baby boy was born to an emperor. When the emperor was standing by the window with his son in his arms, he saw a strange animal in his garden. The emperor immediately called his royal astrologer.

The astrologer said, 'My Lord, this is a Unicorn. It is the most pure and one of the gentlest magical creatures. Unicorns have a horn in the middle of their foreheads. They live for one thousand years, but they will only appear when a worthy ruler is born or is about to die.'

The emperor was happy to hear this. The whole kingdom celebrated the worthy prince's birth with joy!

JANUARY 29

The Brave Prince

Once, there was a brave prince.

One winter, his kingdom was attacked by a frightening creature. The front of its body was of a lion; the middle of a goat and back of a dragon. Besides, it had the heads of all three animals. It also breathed fire.

After it had eaten, the magical creature went up to his home in the mountains. Listening to the troubles of his people, the prince decided to kill the creature.

The prince ran after the creature, up the mountain. He lashed at the creature with his swords. The fairies and eves, who were the creature's slaves, also helped the prince. Soon, they all killed the creature. The people rejoiced and praised the prince for his bravery.

JANUARY 30

The Phoenix's Feather

Once, a princess fell gravely ill. The king asked the witch of the forest to cure her.

The witch said, 'The princess suffers from a rare ailment. To prepare her medicine, I need a Phoenix feather. It is giant bird which lives for a thousand years. Then, it dives into a fire and is reborn from its ashes. It lives on the tallest tree up in the mountains.'

The King travelled far and wide. At last, he saw a Phoenix. With much difficulty, he picked a feather from its nest.

The witch's medicine cured the princess, who thanked her loving father!

JANUARY 31

Snow White and the Seven Dwarfs

Snow White was a beautiful princess. Her stepmother had a Magical Mirror which said, 'You are the fairest of all!'

One day, it said, 'Snow White is the fairest of all!'

The wicked stepmother sent Snow White to the forest, with a soldier, commanding him, 'Soldier, bring her heart back!'

But, the soldier freed her. Deep in the forest, Snow White reached the cottage of the Seven Dwarfs.

The Seven Dwarfs let her stay with them.

Her stepmother learnt about it. She got very angry. Disguised as an old woman, the stepmother convinced Snow White to eat her poisoned apple and she fainted.

The Dwarfs placed her in a glass coffin till a prince kissed her and woke her. The prince and Snow White were happily married.

FEBRUARY 1

Amber and Angus

Once, a king and his queen were sailing back to their country. But a fierce storm wrecked the ship. The king took the queen to a nearby island. They lived there for many years.

One day, the queen gave birth to twins. The fairies of the island helped the queen and took care of her. Amber was the first born and Angus was her brother, born next.

The children grew up with the fairies, learning archery, hunting, swimming, music, poetry, healing and medicine from them.

When they grew up, the children went to their homeland and became its worthy rulers.

FEBRUARY 2

Sacred Animal

Long ago, a herd of stags lived in a thick forest.

One day, Goddess Artemis visited the forest fairy and said, 'I need your help in choosing an animal that will represent me.'

The forest fairy showed the goddess all the animals in the forest but she was not satisfied. The goddess said, 'I represent animals, children, chastity and hunting. So, I want a right candidate.'

The Forest fairy said, 'Then, the stags would be the animals for you!'

The goddess was happy and gave the stags golden antlers and hooves. Since then, the Stags are sacred to the goddess.

FEBRUARY 3

The Pot of Gold

Once, a leprechaun was working hard, trying to hide his pot of gold at the end of a rainbow.

Two brothers, John and Jasper, were gathering wood in the forest. They accidentally saw the leprechaun.

Jasper excitedly screamed, 'That is a leprechaun!'

John said, 'Did you know that if someone catches and holds on to a leprechaun, then he has to give his pot of gold to that person?'

Then, they plotted to catch the leprechaun quietly from behind.

But the leprechaun was too clever for the brothers. He disappeared with his pot of gold before they could catch him!

FEBRUARY 4

The Griffin's Nest

Long ago, four naughty goblins were punished several times by the fairy queen.

Once again they planned to play a prank on someone. One of them said, 'Let's go up to the mountain and steal gold from the griffin's nest.'

Another goblin said, 'Don't you know how strong a griffin is? She has a head, claws and wings of an eagle, and the body of a lion.'

The third goblin said, 'But she always lines her nest with gold!'

The fourth goblin said, 'It is better not to mess with the strong griffin.'

Then, the goblins decided to trick someone else!

FEBRUARY 5

Princess Medina

Once, a beautiful princess called Medina had a pretty complexion and lovely long hair. She sang melodiously and wrote wonderful poetry.

Many suitors came to marry Medina. But she always insulted them saying, 'I am too good for you!'

Fairy Godmother had warned Medina about her pride. But Medina did not listen.

So, Fairy Godmother sent a brave knight who took Medina away and kept her in a thick forest.

There, Medina lived a difficult life and learnt to be humble. She saw that the knight was a good man. She fell in love with him and married him.

FEBRUARY 6

Pegasus and the Prince

Long ago, a brave Prince saved the Cloud Kingdom from a frightening Ogre. Grateful, the Cloud Queen granted a wish to the Prince.

The Prince said, 'I wish to have Pegasus for a day.'

The Prince's close friend asked, 'Who is Pegasus?'

The Prince replied, 'He is a magical White Horse with large wings. The Cloud Queen and Cloud Fairies ride on him.'

The Cloud Queen gave the prince Pegasus for a day.

Pegasus said, 'Brave Prince, you saved our kingdom. I will be more than happy to let you ride on me.'

The Prince rode the whole day and never forgot his experience.

FEBRUARY 7

The Three Ogre Sisters

Long ago, three Ogre sisters lived on top of a mountain. They had teeth and claws made of brass, which made them ugly and frightening.

When they were hungry, the Ogres came down the mountain and took away cattle and little children.

A Magician was sent to slay the Ogres. He thought of a clever trick and said, 'I have come to marry one of you. But I can't decide who is the most beautiful of you three.'

The Ogres fought with each another to marry the Magician. Then, as the three sisters fought, the Magician put a potion on them and turned them into stones.

FEBRUARY 8

The Grotesques

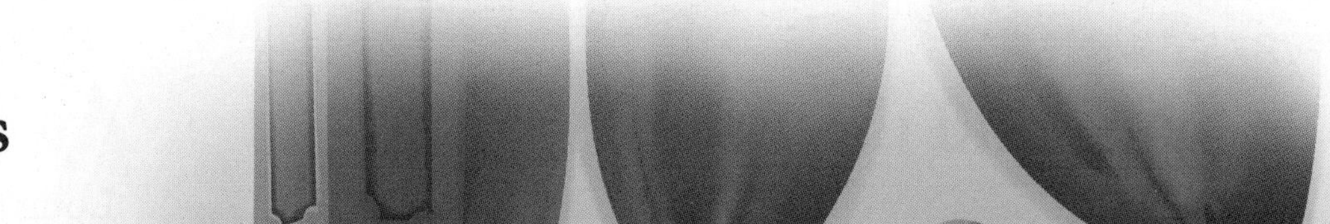

Once, a King was troubled by Seven Witches who came at night, flying on their brooms. The King announced, 'Anyone who will help me get rid of the Seven Witches will be rewarded with precious gems.'

A wise Old Man, who lived in the outskirts of the forest, whispered a solution in his grandson's ear.

The young boy met the King and said, 'Carve Grotesques or Monsters outside your castle walls. They will serve to scare away the Witches.'

The King did as he was told. Magically, the Witches stopped coming to the castle! The King handsomely rewarded the boy.

FEBRUARY 9

Nordur and Skade

Once, there lived a handsome Dwarf Prince named Nordur. He was the guardian of the sea, winds, fire and weather. He loved to wear a crown of sea shells and dress in green.

Skade, a Dwarf Princess of the neighbouring kingdom, was the guardian of winter. Nordur wanted to marry Skade. But she was not interested at all.

Nordur asked the Fairy Godmother to help him and said, 'My love for Skade is true.'

So, the Fairy Godmother blessed Nordur to be the guardian of summer.

Skade was impressed as Fairy Godmother had blessed him.

Nordur married Skade at last!

FEBRUARY 10

The Hippogriff

Long ago, two leprechauns brought a baby hippogriff to Fairyland.

The Fairy Godmother warned them not to keep the hippogriff there but the leprechauns did not agree.

In a few weeks, the hippogriff grew up to be a large animal with the head of an eagle and body of a horse. He started destroying fairy houses as he flew about.

The Fairy Godmother commanded, 'Leprechauns, take him to the mountains as hippogriffs prefer to live in the snow!'

The leprechauns were sorry for causing trouble. They at once led the hippogriff to the mountains safely and never disobeyed Fairy Godmother again.

FEBRUARY 11

Sally and her Grandpa

Little Sally loved reading about magical creatures. When she never understood about something, she went to ask her Grandpa.

One day, Sally sat with her Grandpa and asked, 'Grandpa, what are Trolls?'

Grandpa said, 'Trolls are frightening magical beings. There are Mountain Trolls who look like large piles of stone, Cave Trolls that look like men covered in dirt and Forest Trolls that look like trees. When exposed to sunlight, Trolls turn to stone.'

Sally said, 'I wish to see one!'

Her Grandpa chuckled, 'Oh no! Can you guess what may happen, then?'

Sally laughed aloud and continued reading her book.

FEBRUARY 12

Frey, the Dwarf Leader

Once, the dwarves declared, 'Whoever saves us from the ogres will be our next king.'

Frey, a young dwarf, left home to find weapons.

As he reached the ocean, he helped the Ocean King find his lost daughter. The Ocean King gave him a large magical ship that could be folded.

Then Frey saved many trees from being cut, so the Forest King gave him an invisible unicorn which could travel through air, water or earth.

Frey sailed to the ogres' homes on his ship and then, flying on the unicorn, killed them all.

Thus, Frey became the Dwarf King.

FEBRUARY 13

Sarah and the Pixie

Sarah had a beautiful flower garden.

One spring, her garden was full of sweet smelling flowers. The fragrance of the flowers drew all kinds of insects and birds to Sarah's garden.

One day, Sarah noticed a hawk flying with something in its paws. Sarah shouted, 'Go away! Whom are you hurting?'

Alarmed, the hawk threw something under a toad stool. As she bent down, a tiny boy cried, 'I am a pixie, please help me. I am hurt.'

Sarah lovingly carried the pixie to her house and nursed his wounds.

The pixie thanked Sarah and promised to visit her again.

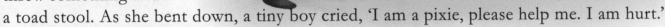

FEBRUARY 14

The Two Rabbits

Once upon a time, there lived two rabbits; one of them white and the other black. They were best friends.

An evil Witch wanted to capture the beautiful Rabbits and lock them away in her castle.

One day, she magically appeared before them and said, 'I will capture you both.'

The Rabbits were scared. The Black Rabbit thought of a plan. He ran and bit the Witch. The evil Witch flew after the Black Rabbit but he disappeared in the darkness. She fell in a deep well and died.

Thus, the brave Rabbit saved his and his friend's life.

FEBRUARY 15

The Magical Swan

Once upon a time, there lived an Old Man. He was the keeper of the city lake. He was very kind and helpful.

One day, a Baby Swan fell in front of the Old Man's house. He saw that it was hurt. The Man took care of the Baby Swan and soon it was well again.

The Swan grew up to be a beautiful white one. One night, the Swan said to the Old Man, 'You have been very kind to me. I will repay your kindness.'

The Swan disappeared and there appeared a heap of gold in its place.

FEBRUARY 16

Three Little Pigs

Three Little Pigs decided to build their own houses.

The first Pig built a house of hay, the second Pig built with sticks, and the third Pig built with bricks.

Soon, a Wolf came by. He huffed and the hay house flew away. The Pig ran to the stick house. The Wolf huffed and puffed. The stick house broke down.

The Pigs ran to the brick house. The Wolf huffed and puffed but nothing happened.

So, he entered the chimney. The Pigs kept boiling water in the fireplace. The Wolf fell straight into it! Burnt, he ran away into the forest!

FEBRUARY 17

The Princess and the Pea

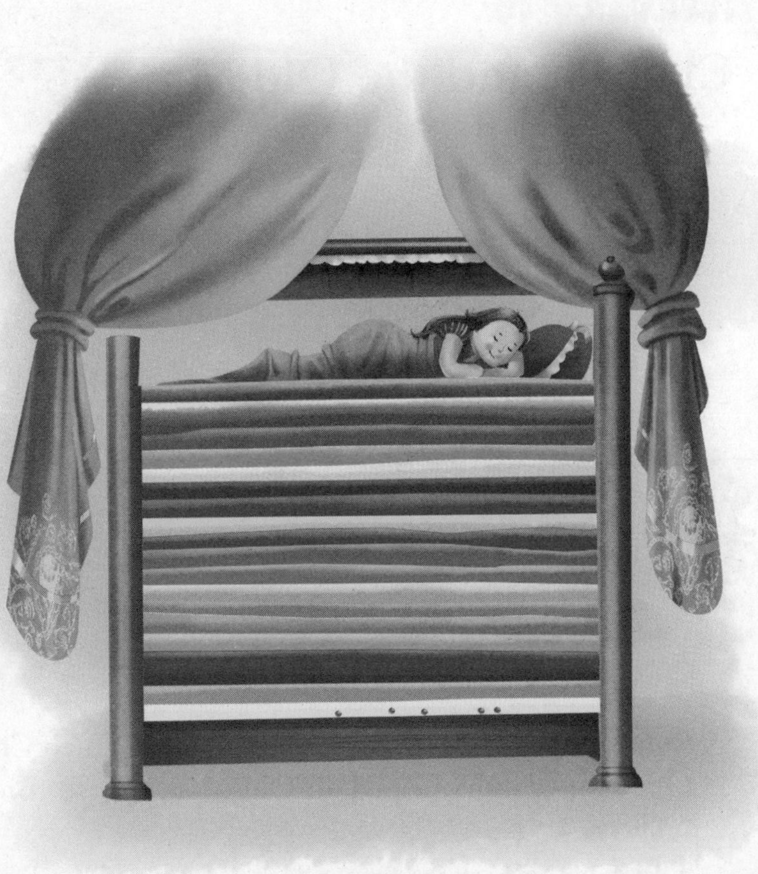

Once, a prince wanted to marry a real princess but he did not find one!

One stormy night, a princess knocked the palace door and said, 'I am a princess. I am lost, please help.'

To test if she truly was a princess, the queen secretly placed peas on her bed. Then, she put twenty mattresses on it.

Next morning, the princess complained, 'I couldn't sleep at all. Something underneath my bed made my back blue.'

The queen exclaimed, 'You are a real princess as you felt the peas through the twenty mattresses!'

The prince and the princess were married.

FEBRUARY 18

The Mirror

Long ago, a girl named Kiara lived with her elder sister.

Close by, lived an ugly witch, whose life was trapped in a magical mirror. This mirror walked to beautiful girls, showed them their ugly reflection and trapped them inside.

One day, Kiara's sister found the mirror. As she saw her ugly reflection, she was trapped, too.

Kiara was watching from afar. She took a club and hit it again and again at the mirror and it broke. The witch died, too. At once, Kiara's sister and many other girls were free!

FEBRUARY 19

Claudia and the Old Man

Once upon a time, there was a little girl named Claudia.

One day, Claudia helped an Old Man, whose foot was stuck in a wood log. He blessed her and went away.

The next day, there was a huge storm. Claudia was going home from school and got stuck on the way.

She then heard a voice, 'Close your eyes.'

She closed her eyes and when she opened them, she saw that she was at home. She looked around and saw the same Old Man who was a Fairy. She thanked him for his help.

FEBRUARY 20

The Rose Flower

A long time ago, there was a beautiful Rose. All the Fairies were very fond of him.

One day, the Rose asked a Fairy to take away all his thorns. He said, 'They make me look ugly!'

The Fairy took away the thorns with magic.

The Rose was very happy. After some time he saw that some insects had started climbing its stalk and wanted to eat him. He cried, 'I want my thorns back! They protected me from the insects.'

The Fairy gave him his thorns back. The insects ran away. He thanked his thorns for helping him!

FEBRUARY 21

The Pine Tree

Once, there was a small Pine Tree. The Tree was very sad because it was small in height.

One day, the Tree saw a little Fairy sitting on a rock. It said, 'Dear Fairy, please make me tall with your magic.'

The Fairy replied, 'If that is what you want then you shall have it.'

With the Fairy's magic the Pine Tree became tall. Sadly, it had to endure fierce winds and rain. The Pine Tree asked the Fairy to turn him back to his original size.

The Pine Tree was happy the way it was and never complained again.

FEBRUARY 22

The Old Woman and the Animals

Long ago, there lived an Old Woman in a forest. She was very kind and loving. She used to feed all the small animals that came to her house.

One day, there was a huge dark storm. The roof of the Old Woman's home was blown away. She became very sad.

The animals thought, 'We must do something for the kind Old Woman.'

They called the Fairies for help. Then, they gathered lots of wood, straws and made a new roof for her. The Old Woman was happy. She thanked the Fairies and the animals and lived happily ever after.

FEBRUARY 23

The Yellow Fish

Once, a young boy used to catch fish from the river to feed his family.

One day, he caught a beautiful Yellow Fish. To his surprise, the Fish pleaded, 'Please let me go. I have little children.'

The Boy felt sad and left the Fish.

On his way back home, the Boy saw something shining in the river. It was the Yellow Fish. The Fish said, 'You were kind to me. I will give reward you!'

It pointed towards a pot of gold on the land. The Boy took the pot home to his family and lived happily ever after.

FEBRUARY 24

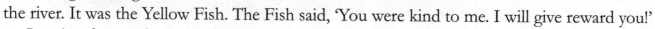

The Brave Little Girl

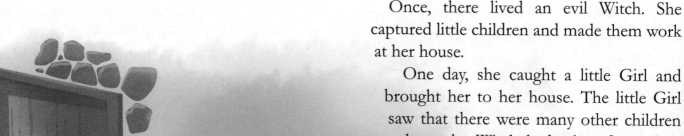

Once, there lived an evil Witch. She captured little children and made them work at her house.

One day, she caught a little Girl and brought her to her house. The little Girl saw that there were many other children whom the Witch had taken from their homes.

She thought of a plan and asked the Witch to come into a small room. The other children locked the door from outside and the little Girl went out from the small window.

They set the house on fire and killed the Witch.

The children thanked the brave Girl and went home happily.

FEBRUARY 25

A Rainy Day

Once, there lived a brother and a sister. They were very fond of each other.

One day, it was raining very heavily. They saw an Ant, which was drowning in the water. They helped the Ant and it thanked them.

While playing in a thick forest the two siblings got lost. It was getting dark and they started crying. Just then, they saw an Ant, which was glowing. They followed the Ant and came out of the forest.

It was the same Ant that they had saved. The Ant was a Pixie in disguise. They thanked the Pixie and went home.

FEBRUARY 26

Rapunzel

Once, a witch stole a baby girl Rapunzel and took her to a tall tower.

Rapunzel had long hair, which the witch used to climb up the tower.

One day, a prince saw the witch climb the tower. When she went away, the prince climbed up the tower with the help of Rapunzel's hair and they fell in love.

When the witch became aware of this, she cut Rapunzel's long hair and sent her to a desert. Then, she blinded the prince.

Years later, the prince heard Rapunzel's song and found her. Her tears healed his blindness and they lived happily thereafter.

FEBRUARY 27

Diamonds and Toads

A beautiful girl lived with her wicked stepmother and stepsister.

One day, while drawing water from the well, the girl offered an old woman water.

The old woman changed into a fairy and blessed, 'Diamonds will fall from your mouth every time you speak.'

When the stepmother heard of this, she sent her daughter to the well. The fairy came as a princess and asked for water. The stepsister rudely refused her. The fairy said, 'Toads will fall every time you speak.'

The angry stepmother threw the girl out of her house. But, she met a prince, who married her.

FEBRUARY 28

Fairies and Ogres

Once, two pretty fairies lived happily in a forest.

Alas, one day, two ogres saw them from their fort and plotted to capture them at night.

The butterflies heard the ogres and informed the fairies.

The fairies remembered that ogres die in bright sunlight.

Thus, the fairies intentionally flew to the ogres' dark fort. The entire night, they flew around, hiding from the ogres.

As the sun rose, the fairies hid behind a curtain on the window. As the ogres entered the room, the fairies drew the curtain. Sunlight fell on the ogres and they died.

The fairies flew back home.

MARCH 1

Jack and the Beanstalk

Jack was a poor boy who lived with his Mother.

One day, when Jack went to sell his cow, a man said, 'Do you need magic beans in exchange for the cow?'

Jack agreed. But his angry Mother threw the beans outside the window. That night, they grew into a giant beanstalk. Jack climbed the beanstalk and reached a rich Giant's house.

Jack stole a bag of gold, a hen that laid golden eggs and a harp before the Giant started chasing him.

Jack climbed down the beanstalk and chopped it, thus, killing the Giant.

Jack was never poor again.

MARCH 2

Wizard and the Brave King

Once, a King banished a Wizard for troubling innocent people. The Wizard said, 'King, I will be back for my revenge.'

The Wizard went up the mountains and lived in a cave for years, studying and practicing magic. Then, he built an army of Sand Giants and sent them to terrorise people.

The people complained, 'The Giants took away our cattle and broke our houses.'

When the Brave King went to the Wizard's cave, he was in front of a cauldron of bubbling potion. He fought the Wizard and threw him in the cauldron, thus, killing him and the Sand Giants.

MARCH 3

The Icy Breath

A long time ago, there lived an old witch. She looked wrinkled and shriveled, but she was strong and powerful.

People were frightened of her as wherever she went, winter followed. She could freeze anything by breathing her icy cold breath on them.

But the old witch had very poor eyesight. Yet, she could foresee and predict future.

One day, she saw that her death was to come from the sea. So, she froze the sea. All the sea creatures were dying.

The brave king of mermaids struck his trident at the chest of the old witch, killing her immediately.

MARCH 4

The Divine Rabbit

It is said that a rabbit lives on the moon. He is called, 'The hare of jade'.

As the story goes this kind rabbit offered himself to be the dinner of the emperor of jade. The fairy godmother was so impressed with him that she blessed him to be divine.

After his death, the divine rabbit was taken by the fairies, in a beautiful pot to live on the moon. The fairies also took the rabbit's help to make the 'Elixir of Immortality' under the shade of a holy tree.

Then, the fairyland folk drank the elixir and lived forever.

MARCH 5

The Wizard and the Harpies

Long ago, the Harpies were a group of mischievous magical women. They had wings like birds and would fly from town to town.

The Harpies loved to steal from people. When they grew tired from their tricks they had powers to spread famine over the land and moved on to the next town.

In a town, a Wizard was very angry when the Harpies stole his horses. He said, 'I will teach you all a lesson so that you shall never trouble anyone again.'

He uttered a powerful spell and turned the Harpies into Bats so they could never hurt anyone!

MARCH 6

The Sorceress and the Giants

Once, there were severe thunderstorms in a vast kingdom that lasted for many days. The King and his sons consulted many astrologers and Wizards. But no one knew the reason for the thunderstorms.

A Prince knew a Sorceress and went to meet her. She said, 'I have been trying to find out about these thunderstorms by my magical sources. The underground Giants are wrestling. That is causing the thunderstorms.'

The Sorceress added, 'You have to send offerings to the Giants to calm them down.'

The Prince, at once, sent fresh fruits and tasty meals for the Giants and the thunderstorms stopped.

MARCH 7

The Mermaid and the Mirror

Long ago, a Mermaid Princess found a beautiful Mirror in ship wreckage under the sea. She thought, 'I haven't seen anything like this before!'

Then, the Mermaid showed it off to her sisters, 'Look at this magical thing I found today.'

When they wanted to touch it, the Mermaid pulled the Mirror away saying, 'I found it. So, it belongs to me.'

When the Mermaid Queen came to know of this, she took away the Mirror, saying, 'This thing is making you proud. One must always be humble and share things.'

The Mermaid apologised and shared the Mirror with everyone.

MARCH 8

The Elves and the Shoemaker

Once, a poor Shoemaker had leather only to make one pair of shoes.

The next morning, he found the finished shoes on the table. Soon, a customer bought them for a good price.

Then, he bought leather to make two pairs of shoes. Again, the two pairs were all finished. He sold them and became a wealthy man.

The Shoemaker and his wife hid behind a curtain and found two Elves working on the shoes.

The Wife said, 'I will make some clothes for the kind Elves.'

When the Elves found the clothes, they wore them and never came back.

MARCH 9

The Woodcutter and the Trees

Some Woodcutters went to the forest to cut wood.

One day, an Old Woodcutter heard someone crying in the forest. When he looked around he saw no one there.

Then, he heard a voice: The Woodcutters will kill us!

The next day, the Old Woodcutter heard crying again. He called out, 'Who are you?'

Just then, two Tree Fairies came to him and said, 'The Trees are crying and whispering. Please do not cut them. If they die, you will too!'

The Old Woodcutter convinced his friends not to cut trees anymore. The Trees were happy and never cried again.

MARCH 10

The Clock in Fairyland

There was a huge Clock in Fairyland that always smiled. He was friendly and never stopped ticking even for a day.

One day, he proudly thought, 'I wake up everyone on time. Without me, they would never get their work done in time. But no one ever acknowledges my work. Let me see how the Magical Folk will get to work on time tomorrow.'

The next day, the Clock stopped ticking for a day.

But the Magical Folk still woke up and went about with the day's work.

The Clock learnt a lesson that one should never be proud!

MARCH 11

The Golden Lake

The Fairies in the Fairyland kept themselves magical and youthful by drinking the water from the 'Golden Lake'.

One day, a Leprechaun named Boofy found some 'Pixie Dust'. So, the other Leprechauns came up with a great plan to steal the water from the Golden Lake. They sprinkled it on the Boofy.

Boofy became a Fairy and crept to the Golden Lake. But the other Fairies were playing near the Lake. They forced Boofy to play with them till midnight. At 12, his true self showed!

The Fairies were very angry with Boofy and he ran away in fear!

MARCH 12

Faye and the Pegasus

One full moon night, Faye saw a beautiful white horse with large wings in her garden. She jumped out of her bed and ran to her window. She gasped, 'Why, it's Pegasus! I read about her in my fairytales all the time.'

Pegasus was enjoying the lush grass in the moonlight.

Faye gathered courage and went out.

Pegasus said, 'Faye, come here. I know you like the magical folk.'

Faye said, 'Will you let me ride you?'

Pegasus agreed and showed Faye all around fairyland.

When they returned, Pegasus promised to take Faye for a ride every full moon.

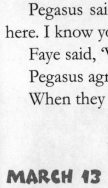

MARCH 13

Fingi

Once, a Woman had no children. She prayed to God day and night for a child.

One day, a Fairy appeared before the Woman. She gave her the seed of a magical plant. When the Woman planted the seed, big roses grew from it. On a big rose sat a little girl, the size of a finger. So, the Woman named her Fingi.

The Woman loved Fingi a lot.

One day, she took her to the Land of Flowers. There, a Prince fell instantly in love with Fingi and married her. After this, they lived happily ever after.

MARCH 14

Cheepi's Magical Hat

Cheepi, the daughter of a Samurai was extremely beautiful and had jewels in her hair.

When the Samurai died, he placed a hat on Cheepi's head. He said, 'This magical hat can only be removed by the person who loves you the most!'

However, everyone made fun of Cheepi as the hat looked ugly. Cheepi was ashamed of it! No matter how hard she tried, she couldn't get rid of it!

One day, a handsome Prince saw Cheepi. He fell in love with her and removed her hat. The hat came off!

Cheepi was very happy and married the Prince.

MARCH 15

The Pencil

It was little Lima's birthday!

Everyone brought lovely gifts for her. Her Grandmother gave Lima a pencil. Lima was surprised, she said, 'Granny, you always give me wonderful things! Today, just a pencil?'

Grandmother smiled and said nothing.

That night, as Lima sat down to finish her homework with the new pencil, a strange thing happened.

The pencil started talking. It said, 'Lima, that's a wrong spelling, try again!'

Lima understood that Grandmother had given her a special and magical pencil.

Lima ran and thanked Grandmother and since then, the pencil has helped Lima learn her spellings and improve her handwriting!

MARCH 16

The Dream

Long ago, a little boy, John, lived with his Brother. The Brother troubled him all day and did not let John study.

One day, John had a test in school. He could not study at all due to his Brother's misbehaviour.

At night, he prayed, 'Fairy Godmother, please help me! I need to pass this test.'

After this, John fell asleep. His Fairy Godmother visited him at night. She placed a hand on his head and blessed him.

The next day, John saw his test paper in the class. Surprisingly, he remembered all the answers. He thanked his Fairy Godmother.

MARCH 17

The Flying Chest

Once, a Man had a strange treasure chest. When he sat in it and twisted its lock, the box would fly up in the air and take him anywhere he wished to go.

One day, the Man flew to a far-off city. There, he heard that the Princess was locked up in a tower by a wicked Magician. So, he flew to the tower and rescued the Princess.

Then, he threw the Magician into the chest. After this, he took him to the ice cold mountains. He left him there.

The people were very happy and praised the Man's bravery.

MARCH 18

A Special Angel

Long ago, cruel demons ruled the world.

They made the men and women work as slaves. Everyone was deeply sad and angry and they stopped believing in God.

However, a little Boy still believed in God. Everyone made fun of him and said, 'If there was a God, He would come to our help!'

The little Boy never listened to them and kept praying.

Then one day, a comet passed over earth. The little Boy said happily, 'God has sent his special Angel to help mankind.'

The Angel landed on earth and killed all the demons.

Everyone believed in God again!

MARCH 19

The Bird-King

Zeus, the king of all living souls called a meeting of the birds. He wanted to appoint a king. All the birds bathed and pressed their feathers and tails to look beautiful. They were all excited.

However, the crow was very sad. He went to a magician and said, 'I am ugly. I will never be appointed the king.'

The magician mumbled some magic words. Instantly, a cloud of beautiful feathers spread around the crow and stuck to him. Now, he looked very beautiful.

Zeus immediately knew that the crow had cheated with fake feathers. So, the crow was disqualified.

MARCH 20

Goldilocks and the Three Bears

Once, three Bears lived in a cottage.

One morning, the Bears went for a walk as their porridge was too hot to eat.

A little lost girl, Goldilocks came to the Bears' cottage. She ate Baby Bear's Porridge as she found the other two bowls either too hot or too cold.

Then, she slept on Baby Bear's bed as she found the other two beds either too hard or too soft.

When they returned, the Baby Bear cried, 'Someone ate my porridge! And someone is sleeping on my bed!'

Goldilocks woke up and ran till she reached her home.

MARCH 21

The Last Song

Omega, a talented singer, had a magical voice.

Once, in a festival in Durin, he won so many jewels and ornaments that he had to hire a ship to take them home.

However, the Sailors on board became jealous of him. So, they attacked him. Omega requested, 'Let me sing one last song before I die.'

The Sailors agreed. As soon as Omega started singing, a dolphin came near the ship. Omega jumped on its back and went safely to the shore.

When the Sailors arrived on the shore, Omega had them arrested and went away with his treasure.

MARCH 22

The Enchanted Rock

Once, Mauris was cutting wood near an oasis. Suddenly, he saw a dust-cloud coming in his direction. He hid behind a dune.

Suddenly, Maurice saw few men coming in his direction. They were robbers and went to a big rock and said, 'Alakazam!'

To Mauris' astonishment, the rock opened and the robbers went in. After a while, they came out and rode away.

Mauris went inside and saw a hidden treasure. He loaded his donkeys with as much treasure as they could carry. After that, he lived a contented life. He used most of the treasure in helping the needy.

MARCH 23

The Snow Fairy

Once upon a time, there lived a little girl named Diana. She was very sweet and helpful. One day, it started snowing heavily. On her way back home, she saw an injured Snow Fairy. The Snow Fairy said, 'I fell down and broke my wing. Will you please help me?'

Diana helped the Snow Fairy and they became good friends. The next day, when Diana was on her way to school, two evil Goblins wanted to catch her. Just then, the Snow Fairy appeared and scared the Goblins away. Diana thanked the Snow Fairy and their friendship became even stronger.

MARCH 24

Hansel and Gretel

Once, a poor Woodcutter lost his two children, Hansel and Gretel in the forest.

The children found a strange house made of bread, cakes, chocolates and candies in the forest. They started eating the house!

Suddenly, an Old Witch came out and caught the children. She locked Hansel in a cage and made Gretel do all the chores.

One day, the Witch said, 'Gretel, heat the oven.'

Gretel could not open the oven door. When the Witch came to help her, Gretel pushed her into the oven and rescued Hansel.

The Children found their way to the house and their father.

MARCH 25

The Evil Ogre

Long ago, there lived an Evil Ogre.

One day, he took away the son of an Ironsmith. The Ironsmith decided to go to the fort of the Evil Ogre and bring back his son.

On his way, he met an Old Woman. She was very old and could not gather fruits from the trees. The Ironsmith said, 'Mother, let me help you.'

The Old Woman thanked him. She told him that to kill the Ogre he must hit him on his head.

The Ironsmith hit the Ogre on his head with a hammer and rescued his son. They went home happily.

MARCH 26

The Friendly Elves

Once upon a time, there lived a girl named Portia. She lived with her mother and two sisters.

One day, Portia's younger sister fell ill.

The Doctor said, 'To save her, you must get the oranges from the Magical Mountain.'

Portia went to the Magical Mountain and met a family of small Elves. She told them interesting stories and was very kind to them. They became fond of the good-natured Portia and gave her the oranges.

Portia went back home and gave the oranges to her sister. Portia's sister was healthy again and they lived happily ever after.

MARCH 27

The Bright Moon

Long ago, an old woman lived in a village.

One night, she saw the moon break into little parts and then get back together.

Then, she noticed that the moon was made of little pixies.

Suddenly, a pixie fell on the ground. The old woman sprinkled water on her and revived her. The pixie gave her a locket.

One day, the old woman fell down while working in the fields. There was no one to help her at that time. So, she opened the locket. Many pixies appeared and took her to her house.

They nursed her back to health.

MARCH 28

The Majestic Unicorn

Long ago, there was a boy named Nate. He lived with his poor mother.

One afternoon, when he was going home, Nate saw a white unicorn in the forest. Nate followed it and saw that hunters were trying to capture it.

Nate started throwing stones at the hunters. They ran after Nate, but he hid in the bushes.

Meanwhile, the unicorn escaped. When the hunters were gone, Nate went home.

Next day, he saw a heap of gold in his lawn. He understood that it was a gift from the unicorn.

Nate and his mother lived happily ever after.

MARCH 29

The Enchanted Sea

Once, there was a brave sailor named Charles. He had sailed all the oceans and seas.

One evening, while Charles was sailing home, a huge storm struck the sea. The ship was wrecked and Charles started drowning.

Just then, he saw a beautiful mermaid. She saved his life and disappeared into the water.

Charles fell in love with her. He sailed the oceans to find her.

One day, Charles saw that the mermaid was being chased by a dangerous shark. Charles bravely killed the shark and married her. The mermaid gave up her tail and lived with him on land.

MARCH 30

Brave Ian

Once upon a time, there lived a brother and a sister, Ian and Kathie. One day while playing in the forest, Kathie went inside a giant's house.

The giant was very wicked. He locked Kathie in his basement. Ian thought, 'If I can trap the giant in the nearby cave, I will be able to save Kathie.'

He threw stones on the giant's windows. The giant chased him into a cave. Ian, cleverly, ran out and pulled a small stone from the cave's roof and big stones started falling. The giant was trapped.

Ian saved Kathie and they went home.

MARCH 31

The Lamp and the Sword

Isaac had a magic lamp. When he rubbed it, a castle appeared.

One day, an old man begged Isaac for food.

Isaac rubbed the lamp and the magic castle appeared. Isaac invited the old man inside and fed him various delicacies.

The old man said, 'I am a wizard and came here to test you. I will give you a magic sword for your kindness.'

Isaac thanked the man.

Sometime later, a large army attacked Isaac's kingdom. The king's army was losing. Isaac used his magic sword to defeat them. The pleased king married his daughter to Isaac.

APRIL 1

The Little Mermaid

Once, a Mermaid saved a Prince from a wrecked ship. But before he could wake up, she left. He only remembered her sweet song.

But the Mermaid was in love with the Prince and gave up her voice in exchange of legs.

A Witch warned her, 'You will never be able to return back to the sea.'

When the Mermaid met the Prince, she could not express that she loved him.

Meanwhile the Prince was getting married to a Princess. The Mermaid was very sad. She left the palace but the Prince brought her and married her instead.

APRIL 2

The Princess' Spell

Once, a wicked Sorcerer fell in love with a Princess. He cast a spell on her.

Every night, the Princess got up at midnight. Under the spell, she entered a secret passage in the wall. The Sorcerer waited for her at the end of the passage and danced with her all night.

Despite repeated efforts, no one was able to find where the Princess disappeared at night. So, the distressed King went to a Fairy and asked her for help. The Fairy removed the Princess' spell.

In return, the King married the Princess to the Fairy's Grandson.

APRIL 3

Sleeping Beauty

Once, a king was blessed with a baby girl. He threw a grand feast and invited six fairies, but forgot to invite the seventh fairy.

During the feast, five fairies blessed the princess. Suddenly, the seventh fairy appeared, and cursed the princess, 'She will die when sixteen.'

But the sixth fairy blessed, 'She will only sleep for hundred years.'

At sixteen, the princess touched a spinning wheel's needle and fell into deep sleep. Everyone in the kingdom slept with her.

After a hundred years, a prince came and kissed the princess. Suddenly, everyone was awake!

The prince and the princess were happily married.

APRIL 4

The Rain of Stars

Once, a poor little girl was walking on the road at night. She saw an old woman shivering in the cold and offered the old woman her jacket.

Then, the little girl saw a boy crying because of the cold. The kind girl gave her scarf to him.

In this manner, she gave most of her clothes to people who needed them more.

The fairies were pleased with her kindness. They caused the stars to rain down and form a sparkling cloak around her. The moon rested on her head like a crown.

Thus, the little girl became very famous in her village.

APRIL 5

The Crystal Ball

Once, a ship carrying a crystal ball as a gift to the Emperor of China got caught in a storm and sank. The King sent the best of his divers to recover the crystal ball. However, none of them ever returned.

A Woman requested the King to let her try. In reality, she was a powerful Sorceress. The King agreed.

The Sorceress tied a rope around her waist and dived to the bottom of the sea. There, a fierce sea-monster was guarding the crystal ball.

Using her powers, the Sorceress killed the monster and came back with the crystal ball.

APRIL 6

Thumbelina

A farmer's wife planted a corn given by a witch to have children. A tiny girl came out of its flower and she was named Thumbelina.

One night, a frog carried Thumbelina away as a bride for her son. But with the help of a butterfly, Thumbelina escaped.

It was winter and a mouse gave Thumbelina shelter. She soon found a sick swallow and nursed him to health.

The mouse suggested, 'Thumbelina, marry my rich neighbour, the mole.'

Thumbelina refused and flew away with the swallow.

Thumbelina then met a flower fairy and married him. They lived happily ever after.

APRIL 7

The Fawn

Once, a young girl and her brother lived with a witch. She made them do all the chores. When the brother rebelled, she turned him into a fawn.

One day, the fawn wandered away into the forest. A prince was hunting there. He followed the fawn into the witch's house.

Seeing the young girl in the witch's house, the prince was captivated by her beauty and befriended her. He learnt her sad story and killed the witch.

The minute the witch died, the fawn turned back into a boy. Then, the prince married the girl and they all lived happily.

APRIL 8

Beauty and the Beast

Once, a merchant was caught in a storm. He entered a castle nearby but there was no one there. However, he was served a lavish dinner. Then, while wandering in the garden, he plucked a rose for his daughter, Beauty.

A beast lived in the castle, who growled, 'If you want me to spare your life, bring your daughter here.'

Beauty became friends with the beast. One day, she went to see her father. When Beauty returned, the beast was dying. She exclaimed, 'Oh, I love you!'

Lo! The beast turned into a prince as a witch's spell that was on him broke. They were happily married.

APRIL 9

The Sea-Dragon

In a coastal town, people lived a fearful life. A terrible Dragon lived in the sea. Many a times, it suddenly jumped out of the sea and threatened people working or playing on the beach.

Seeing this, the Goddess of Happiness felt bad. She thought, 'This Dragon is angry only because he is all alone. I must do something.'

So, she came to Earth and summoned the Dragon. Then, she changed his heart and filled it with love and happiness.

Now, the Dragon became a peaceful creature. He began to play with the children on the beach and lived happily amongst them.

APRIL 10

The Gnome

Once, a Woodcutter saved a Gnome's life. In return, the Gnome gave him a lot of gold.

So, the Woodcutter became rich and went to marry the Princess.

On hearing the Woodcutter's desire, the King said, 'I can marry my daughter to you on one condition. You will have to build a boat which can sail on both land and water.'

The Woodcutter promised the King and left. Then, he went to the Gnome for guidance. The Gnome built a boat with wheels and solved the problem.

Seeing the boat, the King was pleased and married his daughter to the Woodcutter.

APRIL 11

The Tale of the Turnip

Once, two brothers lived in a village. The Elder Brother was rich and the Younger Brother was poor.

One day, the Younger Brother said to the Elder Brother, 'Please help me to start a business.'

He replied, 'I don't want to give you a single penny.'

Hearing this, the Younger Brother sadly went to the nearby wood.

There, he met a Pixie. With his help, he grew a huge turnip and decided to gift it to the King.

The King was pleased to see the enormous turnip. In return, he gave the Younger Brother gold coins and made him rich.

APRIL 12

Father Christmas

Once, there lived a poor orphan named Manny. He did not have anyone to celebrate festivals with.

On Christmas Eve, he went to sleep early. At midnight, he heard some noise near the chimney. He ran out of his room and peeped outside.

He saw a man in red clothes with a huge white beard. He was carrying a sack on his back. It was Santa Claus!

Santa Claus filled Manny's room with gifts. He gave Manny chocolates and cookies to eat. He promised, 'Manny, I will celebrate Christmas with you every year.'

Manny was never alone on Christmas again.

APRIL 13

Maura's Groom

Once, a beautiful Princess, Maura, wanted to marry a genuine and good human being.

An Elf guarded Maura. One day, he said to her, 'I have a good plan to find a good match for you. Dress as a beggar. Marry the man who treats a beggar with respect and gives her food.'

Maura did as directed by the Elf. She begged for days. Finally, a Sheikh laid out a lavish dinner and treated her with sympathy.

Seeing his generosity towards a poor woman, Maura decided that he was the most righteous and noble man. So, she married him.

APRIL 14

Princess in the Lake

Long ago, a Queen gave birth to a Princess.

One day, a Magician saw her. He was enchanted by her beauty. So, he carried and hid her deep inside a lake.

The King tried to find her but failed. So, he went to a brave Knight and asked for help. The Knight knew a Witch and took her help. She said, 'You will have to drink the water of the entire lake to find the Princess.'

With the Witch's magical powers, the Knight emptied the lake and rescued the Princess.

The King gave him one thousand gold coins as a reward.

APRIL 15

The Brave Cloud

Once upon a time, there lived an Ogre called Grams. He used to capture little Fairies and lock them in a bottle.

One day, Grams caught a little Fairy who was the best friend of a Cloud.

The Cloud was very sad. He decided to rescue his Fairy friend. He asked Father Cloud to give him the power to rain down whenever he wanted.

So, wherever the Ogre went, the Cloud poured rain over him. The Ogre became irritated and finally gave up. He freed the Fairy and apologised to her. He swore never to trouble anybody ever again.

APRIL 16

The Sea Nymphs

Once upon a time, there was a very just and kind king.

One day, the king decided to sail across the sea to meet his sister. On his way, the king's ship was attacked by pirates. They tried to attack and loot the ship.

The king prayed to the sea nymphs, 'If I have ever been kind to my people and never cheated anybody, then please help me.'

The sea nymphs heard his prayer and drowned the pirates.

The king was very thankful. He promised to always be kind to everyone and went on his way to meet his sister.

APRIL 17

The Rainbow Lights

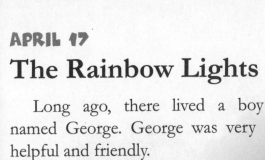

Long ago, there lived a boy named George. George was very helpful and friendly.

One day when George was taking his dog Casper for a walk, he saw a group of Pixies. He thought, 'Wow, these Pixies are so colourful! If I capture them then I can see them every day.'

George went close to them and they were frightened. He felt sorry and went back home.

The next night, when George looked out of his window, he saw the rainbow lights! It was the colourful Pixies!

George understood that the Pixies were more beautiful while free than captured.

APRIL 18

The Magical Butterfly

Long ago, there lived a Prince. He was very handsome and kind. He helped all his people and was liked by everybody. However, he was very lonely.

One day, while hunting in the forest the Prince saw a little Caterpillar. It was in its covering, waiting to become a butterfly. A small branch was going to fall on it. The Prince cut the branch and saved the Caterpillar.

Suddenly, he saw a bright light coming from the covering. A beautiful Princess came out of the cocoon. The Prince fell in love with her. They were married and lived happily ever after.

APRIL 19

The Blue Deer

Once upon a time, there lived a brave Hunter.

One day the Hunter saw a bright blue deer. The deer was so beautiful that the Hunter decided not to kill him.

The Hunter moved on to the next forest. There he saw a wild pig. When he was shooting at it, he did not see that a Lion stood behind him.

When the Lion was going to jump on the Hunter, the blue deer appeared! The Lion was surprised and ran away.

The Hunter saw what had happened. He thanked the deer and swore never to hurt innocent animals again.

APRIL 20

The Helpful Elf

Once upon a time, there lived an Old Man.

One day, the Old Man met a hungry Elf. He gave the Elf a loaf of bread.

The next day, the Old Man saw the little Elf again. He again gave him food. The Elf and the Old Man became good friends.

One day, some robbers stole all of the Old Man's food. The Old Man was very sad. He thought, 'Now I have nothing to give the little Elf.'

Just then he saw the little Elf with lots of food. The Old Man thanked him and they enjoyed the food together.

APRIL 21

True Love

Long ago, a beautiful princess lived in her castle. Her prince, who was her true love, was under the spell of a wicked witch. He had forgotten all about the princess.

The princess was sad.

One day, a swallow said, 'You must burn the rose that the wicked witch keeps her magic in.'

The princess went to the witch's fort and said, 'I have the most beautiful rose in the world.'

The witch became jealous and showed her rose. The princess burned the rose and thus the witch lost her magic. The prince was saved and he married the princess.

APRIL 22

The Chocolate House

Once upon a time, there was an evil Ogre. The Ogre had a magical power which was stored in his house that was completely made of chocolate. He used to lock away the children who entered the chocolate house.

Once, a little Boy and his Sister entered the house. They saw the Ogre and were very afraid. The Ogre said, 'Now you are trapped!'

The Boy thought of a plan. He lit a huge fire and the house started melting. They quickly ran out of the house and the Ogre was killed.

They safely went back home to their mother.

APRIL 23

The Fantasy Island

Once upon a time, there lived a little girl named Serena. She was very helpful.

One day, she heard that a wicked witch had taken away her friend's little sister to a fantasy island.

Serena decided to help her friend. On her way, she met a fairy. Serena was very friendly and the fairy became her friend.

When Serena reached the island, she took her friend's sister out of the witch's castle.

The fairy took them back home and destroyed the island's bridge. The witch was trapped on the island forever.

Everybody thanked Serena and the fairy for their bravery.

APRIL 24

Mila's Coat

A girl, Mila, had a magical red coat. It had the power to make the person wearing it invisible.

One day, an evil Witch attacked Mila's village. Everyone was very scared.

A wise woman said, 'Nobody should get out of their homes. Someone must break the Witch's magical crystal ball then she would lose her magical powers.'

Mila thought, 'I must go and break it!'

Then, she wore her coat and went to the Witch's castle. The Witch could not see Mila and Mila broke the crystal ball.

The Witch lost all her powers and never troubled Mila's village again.

APRIL 25

The Silver Cry

Long ago, there lived a beautiful water nymph called Silver Cry. She was named so because of her beautiful voice. Silver Cry loved singing and everybody enjoyed listening to her.

One day, a Sea Monster attacked Silver Cry's people. They started swimming in all the directions. Silver Cry was very sad. She decided to help her people.

She went to the Monster and sang a lullaby. Her voice was so sweet that the Monster fell asleep. They tied the Monster and left it somewhere far away.

Everyone thanked Silver Cry for her bravery and sat down to hear her sing.

APRIL 26

The Mischievous Boy

Once upon a time, there lived a naughty boy. He never listened to his mother.

One afternoon, the boy fell in a big hole. His mother had warned him not to go near that area.

The boy was afraid and started crying. Just then, he saw an elf standing at the opening of the hole. He cried for help.

The elf used his magic and pulled the boy from the hole. The boy thanked the elf and went home.

The boy apologised to his mother for misbehaving. Thereafter, he always listened to his mother and became a good boy.

APRIL 27

The Brave Prince

Long ago there lived a Prince in the kingdom of Chance Harbour. He was very brave and kind. One day, he fell in love with a beautiful Princess.

A wicked Witch had put a curse upon the Princess. As soon as the sun rose, the Princess fell into a deep sleep.

Then, finally, the Prince fought the Witch. However, the Witch was very powerful.

The Prince took his magical sword and killed the Witch. The Witch's evil curse was lifted and the Princess woke up from her sleep.

The Prince and the Princess were married. They lived happily ever after.

APRIL 28

The Magical Shoes

Once upon a time, there was a girl named Blair. She was very poor and lived with her family. One day, while working in the village shop, she saw a little rat.

The rat looked very hungry. Blair gave it cheese to eat. After eating the cheese the rat started to glow! It then turned into Fairy Godmother.

Fairy Godmother said, 'You are a kind girl. I will give you a reward.'

She gave Blair a pair of magical shoes. Wearing those Blair could dance like a fairy. Soon, everyone recognised Blair's talent and she became very famous and rich.

APRIL 29

The Wise Tree

Long ago, there was a tree which could speak. The magical Tree was very old and helped all the village people.

One day, a Boy came to the Tree and said, 'My friend has lost his cat and is very sad. Please tell me what should I do?'

The Tree was very happy with the Boy because he wanted to help his friend. He told the Boy to look under the house stairs.

The Boy looked under the stairs and found the cat with a pot of gold. He thanked the magical Tree and shared the gold with his friend.

APRIL 30

The Lamp and the Sword

Long ago, there was an evil Ogre. He used to trouble the people of a village a lot.

One day a Prince decided to help the people. On his way to the Ogre's den, he saw a Unicorn. The Unicorn's horn was stuck in a bush. The Prince helped the Unicorn. The Unicorn decided to accompany the Prince.

The Prince challenged the Ogre to a horse race. With the help of the Unicorn, the Prince won the race.

The Ogre was defeated and he promised never to trouble the villagers again. Everybody praised the Prince and thanked the Unicorn.

MAY 1

The Witty Prince

Once upon a time, there lived a beautiful Princess. However, she was locked away in a tower by a wicked Witch.

One day, a Prince heard about the sad Princess. He decided to go and save her. The tower was always guarded by an Ogre. The Ogre was very foolish.

The witty Prince decided to trick the Ogre. He ran around the tower and the Ogre followed. The Prince hid in the bushes and the Ogre kept running.

Soon the Ogre was tired and he collapsed. The Prince rescued the Princess. They fell in love and lived happily ever after.

MAY 2

The Eleven Wild Swans

Once, a witch cast a spell on eleven princes and a princess named Elisa. She said, 'You will turn into swans during the day and humans at night!'

But Elisa escaped her spell and the swan princes carried her to another town.

A fairy advised Elisa, 'Knit nettles plants into eleven shirts for your brothers. But do not speak till they are finished.'

The people saw this and they thought Elisa was a witch. They complained to the king. But Elisa finished the eleven shirts and turned her brothers into humans.

The king learnt about Elisa's story and married her.

MAY 3

Bluebeard

Bluebeard was a wealthy man but had an ugly blue beard. He had several wives but no one knew of them. He wanted to marry his neighbour's daughters. The youngest daughter married Bluebeard.

The next day, Bluebeard said, 'Wife, I have to leave on business. Take this bunch of keys. You can go anywhere except the room in the basement.'

But his wife opened the forbidden room and found Bluebeard's previous wives there. A blood stain appeared on the key, magically.

When Bluebeard returned, he tried to kill his wife. But her brothers rescued her and killed Bluebeard.

MAY 4

Puss in Boots

A miller's youngest son received a cat in inheritance while the elder brothers took the mill and the mules.

The cat spoke, 'Master, give me a pair of boots and I will bring great fortunes.'

The cat caught rabbits and went to the king, 'My master, Marquis of Carabas, sends gifts.' Then, he went to an ogre's castle and fooled him to turn into a rat. Quickly, he ate him up.

One day, the king was passing by the castle. The cat said, 'King, this is my master's castle.'

The king was impressed and married his daughter to the master.

MAY 5

The Magical Sphinx

It is said that once a magical being, the sphinx, seized a kingdom.

The sphinx stood at the entrance of the capital city to stop anyone from entering or leaving.

The emperor sent his witty minister to face the sphinx.

Sphinx asked him, 'What animal is that which in the morning goes on four feet, at noon on two, and in the evening upon three?'

The witty minister answered, 'Man crawls on all fours in his infancy, walks on two legs as an adult and walks with a cane in old age.'

The sphinx accepted her defeat and flew away.

MAY 6

The Prince and the Dragon

Long ago, a handsome Prince fell in love with a beautiful Princess. However, an evil Witch took away the Princess and locked her on an island.

The island was guarded by a Dragon. The Dragon used to breathe fire through his nostrils.

The Prince wanted to save the Princess. He sailed to the island and took his magical sword that his Fairy Godmother had given him.

He killed the Dragon and freed the Princess.

The Prince also fought the wicked Witch and killed her. The Prince and the Princess got married and went back home happily.

MAY 7

The Great Escape

Once, the people of the village were troubled by a Sea Monster. The Sea Monster destroyed their crops and their houses.

One day, they prayed to the Fairy Godmother. The Fairy Godmother appeared and said, 'When the Monster will come to your town, together say the word, 'Vanish!'

The next day, the Sea Monster came from the shore again. He started destroying the villager's crops. The villagers shouted together, 'Vanish!' and after a few seconds the Monster vanished!

They were very happy and thanked the Fairy Godmother. The Fairy Godmother said, 'You must always stay together, no one can harm you then!'

MAY 8

The Colourful Kingdom

Once upon a time, there was a kingdom full of different colours. The people of that village were very colourful and friendly.

One day, an evil Magician cast a spell upon the kingdom. All the colours started fading. The people became very sad.

They requested the Wind Fairy to help them. She reversed the evil magic and the colours started shining again. The Fairy defeated the evil Magician and saved the kingdom.

That night the colours shined brighter than they ever had. Everyone in the kingdom celebrated the victory and thanked the Fairy. Good deeds always win over the evil ones.

MAY 9

The Evil Goblins

Once upon a time, there lived a king whose kingdom was troubled by some naughty goblins. They stole from people's houses and created problem for everyone.

One day, the king decided to rid the kingdom of the goblins. He gathered all his people and thought of a plan.

The next day, they gathered all the fruits from the forest at one place. When the goblins came to steal the fruits, they captured them. Then they put the goblins on a ship and sent them to a far away land. The people were happy and praised their intelligent and good king.

MAY 10

Jake and Milo

Once upon a time, there was a boy named Jake. He had a Unicorn named Milo. Jake and Milo were best friends.

One day, some thieves on horses attacked the village. They stole all the goods from the village people. Jake saw this and protested.

The thieves started chasing Jake. He called for Milo and rode very fast. Suddenly, he saw a cliff. Milo jumped high and crossed the gap. However, the thieves all fell down the cliff and died.

The village was saved. The King rewarded Jake and Milo for their bravery and they lived happily ever after.

MAY 11

The Water Fairy

Long ago, there lived a Prince. He was very kind and helpful. One day, the people of the kingdom came to him and said, 'There is no water in the kingdom. If this continues, we will all die of thirst.'

The Prince decided to go in search of the Water Fairy. However, the way to her castle was very dangerous.

The brave Prince sailed the oceans and faced the troubles. When he reached the Fairy's castle he requested her to provide his kingdom with water. She was pleased with his bravery and made it rain. Thus, the kingdom was saved.

MAY 12

The Intelligent Fisherman

Once, a poor Fisherman lived in a small cottage near the sea.

One day, a wicked Witch requested the Farmer, 'I will make you rich. Give me your cottage and I will give you a big house.'

The Fisherman understood that the Witch planned to rule over the sea from his cottage and make him her slave. He said, 'I am happy with what I have. I do not want more.'

The evil Witch went away in anger. Her plan had failed. She swore never to come near that shore ever again.

The Fisherman lived happily in his little cottage.

MAY 13

Jessie saved the Golden Bird

Once, there was girl named Jessie. She used to gather woods in the forest.

One day, Jessie saw a golden bird on a tree. Suddenly, she saw some wicked goblins coming towards the bird.

She thought, 'If the goblins catch the golden bird, they will hurt it. I must do something to warn it.'

Jessie picked some wood and set fire under the tree. When the golden bird saw the smoke under the tree, it became alert.

The goblins, too, became afraid and ran away.

Then, the golden bird dropped a bag of gold on Jessie's basket and flew away.

MAY 14

The Witty Knight

Once, there lived a brave Knight.

One day, the Knight heard a villager say, 'O that Ogre is evil! He troubles us for no reason.'

The brave Knight went to the Ogre's swamp on his horse. The Ogre threatened to eat the Knight.

The Knight told the Ogre that a thorn was stuck on the horse's hooves. If he wanted to eat them, he will have to take it out.

When the Ogre brought his face closer to the ground the Knight made his horse kick the Ogre. The Ogre fell and died. Everybody thanked the Knight and praised him.

MAY 15

The Big House

Once, there lived a boy named Adam. He was very curious.

One day, Adam decided to take a walk along the forbidden land. Soon, he saw a huge wooden house. When he entered the house, he saw that all the furniture was bigger than the usual ones.

Next, he went into the bedroom and saw a giant sleeping on the bed. He gasped out loud.

The giant woke up and started chasing Adam.

Then, suddenly the giant slipped and fell into a deep pit. He died because of his bruises and wounds.

Adam never went to the forbidden land again.

MAY 16

The Golden Wood

Long ago, there lived a boy named Evans in a village. He was very kind and helpful.

One day, while crossing the forest Evans saw an Old Lady.

The Old Lady said, 'Son, please chop some wood for me. I am too old to do it on my own.'

Evans was very tired but he helped the Old Lady. After he had chopped the wood he turned to give the wood to her. He saw that the lady had turned into a Fairy.

The Fairy rewarded him for his kindness. The wood log turned into gold and Evans became rich.

MAY 17

The Clever Cat

Long ago, there lived a girl named Jenna. She had a cat which could do magic. One day, some robbers tried to attack the village leader.

Jenna was scared and wanted to help the village leader. Suddenly, she saw that her cat had started glowing! The cat soon turned into a huge Tiger.

The robbers saw the Tiger and ran away. The Cat then got to its original size and said, 'Jenna, you have always taken care of me. I will protect and help you.'

Jenna was very happy. The village leader rewarded her in front of the whole village.

MAY 18

Faye and Elmore

Once, there lived a girl named Faye.

One day, while going to school she saw a Dragon. A thorn had pierced the Dragon's foot.

Faye helped him and the Dragon said, 'My name is Elmore. You were kind to me, now I will always help you.'

After a few days, an evil Magician attacked the village. He started destroying all the houses. Elmore came and whispered a plan into Faye's ear.

Faye challenged the Magician to float in air. As the Magician flew, Elmore caught hold of him.

He killed the Magician and saved the village. Everybody thanked Elmore and Faye.

MAY 19

The Evil Ogress

Long ago, a Prince was crossing the forest. Just then, he saw a Girl who begged him, 'Will you please take me home?'

The Prince pulled her on his horse.

On their way, the Girl asked the Prince to stop the horse. She wanted to drink water. After some time had passed the Prince decided to go after her. He saw the true reflection of the Girl in water. She was an Ogress who wanted to eat him!

He came back to his horse and waited. When the Ogress came back he killed her with his sword and went back home safely.

MAY 20

The Two Brothers

Once, there lived two brothers named William and Fredrick. Their village was on the shore of a vast ocean. One day, a sea monster cntered their city and started destroying everything.

William thought of a plan. He tied a huge fish with a rope and with his horse. He dragged it towards the ocean. The monster followed him.

While William was distracting the monster, Fredrick tied the monster's feet.

When the monster tried to chase after Fredrick, it fell.

The villagers then threw the monster from a high cliff into the sea where it died. Thus, the village was saved.

MAY 21

The Dragon Born

Once upon a time there lived a boy named Gray. He was raised by a good-spirited Dragon. Gray was a good warrior.

One day, an evil Witch took over the forest. All the creatures of the forest were very scared. They all went to the Dragon and said, 'O mighty Dragon, please save us from the wicked Witch.'

Just then, Gray decided to go and fight the Witch. He took the magical spear that a Pixie had given him and defeated the Witch.

All the creatures were very happy and praised the brave-hearted Gray. The Dragon was very proud.

MAY 22

The Flying Chair

Long ago, there lived a kind and humble Old Woman. However, because of her age, she used to have trouble walking around.

One day, a Fairy came in the shape of a cat. She went to the Old Woman and begged for food. The Old Woman smiled and gave the cat some milk.

This continued for two days. The Old Woman was always very generous and fed the cat.

The Fairy was very happy with the Woman's behaviour. She gave her a flying chair that could take her anywhere. The Old Woman was never troubled because of old age.

MAY 23

The Little Bird Pixies

Once upon a time, there lived a group of Pixies. They would often take the shape of a bird and fly around. They were very cheerful.

One day, an evil Witch saw them and said, 'If I capture these Pixies, then I will steal their magic!'

A little Girl, who didn't have feet, heard the Witch's plan. She warned the Pixies about the evil Witch. The Pixies used their combined magic and locked away the Witch.

As a reward for her help they gave the Girl the blessing of flying. The Girl happily flew around, helping anyone she could!

MAY 24

The Emperor's New Clothes

A vain Emperor, who loved wearing new clothes, hired two Con Men.

They promised, 'Your Majesty, We weave the finest clothes from a fabric which is invisible to only foolish people.'

The foolish Emperor agreed.

Finally, one day, the Con Men reported that they had finished a suit for the Emperor and pretended to dress him. The Emperor marched in a procession before his subjects. They pretended to play along as they did not want to appear foolish.

A child laughed, 'But the Emperor is wearing nothing at all!' Everyone heard him and started laughing. The foolish Emperor ran back in embarrassment!

MAY 25

The Mango Tree

Once upon a time, there was a magical Mango Tree. The fruits that grew on the Tree were made of gold.

One day, a Merchant passed through that way. He saw the Tree and was amazed. He said, 'Dear Tree, I am very hungry. Please give me a ripe mango to eat.'

The Tree dropped a golden mango. The Merchant said, 'I don't want gold, just a real mango!'

The Tree was happy that the merchant was not greedy for gold, so he gave him mangoes to eat. Also, he rewarded him with many golden mangoes for his pure heart.

MAY 26

Katherine and the Frog

Katherine was an obedient and kind girl.

One day, while playing in her garden, Katherine saw that an ugly frog was stuck in a bush and nobody wanted to help it.

Katherine helped the frog and left it in the water stream. The frog started to grow. She then took it and left it in the lake. However, it had grown bigger till then.

Katherine then left it in the ocean. The frog magically turned into a sea nymph and said, 'Thank you for your kindness.'

She gave Katherine a magical stone, which fulfilled wishes, and then vanished into the water.

MAY 27

The Fountain of Love

Long ago, Sam and Samantha lived with their wicked Aunt. She made them work all day long.

One day, the children were chopping wood in the forest. Suddenly, a magical fountain appeared and a musical voice said: 'This is the Fountain of Love. Whoever drinks from it becomes a loving person!'

The Children were overjoyed. They filled their bottles with the water and ran home. There, they said to their Aunt, 'It's a magical drink!'

Their Aunt was curious so she drank it. Lo! The next minute, she became loving and kind to them.

They all lived happily ever after.

MAY 28

The Blessed Fairy

Once upon a time, a kind Fairy was blessed that fire or heat could never burn her.

A little girl named Riana was the Fairy's friend.

One day, a wicked Magician came to the village. He saw Riana and thought, 'If I catch her, she can be my slave forever.'

The Fairy came to know of his plans. She challenged the Magician to chase and catch her.

The proud Magician flew after her on his broom. The Fairy flew closer and closer to the sun.

Nothing happened to her but the Magician was burned. Thus, she saved Riana's life!

MAY 29

The Magical Ring

Long ago, there lived two sisters, Laura and Lisa. They were very fond of each other. Laura had a magical ring that could grant all her wishes.

One day, a Witch saw the two sisters playing in the forest. She saw Laura rub her ring and knew that the ring was magical.

The Witch decided to take the ring from Laura. She captured Lisa and said, 'Give me the ring or else I will kill her.'

Laura loved her sister. She threw the ring in the well and the Witch jumped after it and drowned. The sisters went home happy.

MAY 30

The Blue Bottle Bird

Once, there was a blue bottle bird named Beez. He was very helpful and kind.

One day, an Evil Magician decided to cut down the forest where Beez lived.

All the animals were very sad.

Beez encouraged everyone to do something! Just then, he saw a Fairy drowning in the water. He flew and saved the Fairy.

The Fairy said, 'Thank you for saving my life. I will grant you a wish.'

Beez asked the Fairy to help him protect the forest. The Fairy called other Fairies and they all drove away the Magician.

Beez's kind deed saved the forest!

MAY 31

The Friendly Elves

One day, a Rabbit was looking for food in a garden. He found a large field of carrots and began to eat them.

Suddenly, a large Dog appeared and growled at him. He said, 'You look so fat and juicy. I'm going to eat you.'

The Rabbit, although scared, did not panic. He said, 'Dear Dog, let me eat carrots first. I'll be juicier then.'

The foolish Dog agreed. Seeing the opportunity, the Rabbit prayed to the Sleep Fairy, 'Dear Fairy, please help me!'

Hearing the prayer, the Sleep Fairy made the Dog sleep while the innocent Rabbit ran away.

JUNE 1

Hop o' My Thumb

A poor Woodcutter had seven sons. His youngest son, Hop o' My Thumb, was as tiny as a thumb, but he was clever.

One day, the Woodcutter left his sons in the forest as he had no food. Hop took his brothers to a Giant's house and asked for food from the Giant's kind wife.

When the Giant returned, he said, 'I smell humans. Are you hiding them?'

The kind wife said, 'You must be dreaming!'

That night, she gave Hop a huge pot of gold, and helped him run back home.

Hop and his family were never poor again!

JUNE 2

Snow White and Rose Red

Snow White and Rose Red lived in a forest. One night, a bear asked them for shelter. The sisters said, 'Please come in.'

The next day, they saw a dwarf in the forest. His beard was stuck in a tree trunk. The sisters cut his bread and freed him.

But the dwarf attacked them, saying, 'You ruined my beard!'

Before the dwarf could harm them, the bear attacked him.

Immediately, the bear turned into a prince! A wicked dwarf had cast a spell on him, which was finally broken.

The sisters were surprised, but happy. The three lived happily together.

JUNE 3

A Brother and Sister

Once, a Brother and Sister left home, because their Stepmother was a Witch and troubled them.

They did not know she had cast a spell on all lakes and ponds. Tired and thirsty, the Brother drank from a lake. And he became a Deer!

The sister took care of him, until one day, a King came hunting the Deer and fell in love with the Sister. They were soon married.

The Sister told the King everything. The King killed the Witch and the Brother became human again. Thus, the King, his Wife and her Brother lived happily for many years.

JUNE 4

Donkey Skin

Once, a king wanted to marry a beautiful princess. But she said, 'I will only marry you if you can do all the things I ask you to.'

First, she asked for a dress as the colour of the sky, moon and sun.

The king used magical powers and gave her the dress.

But the princess wanted to test him further and hid in the neighbouring country, wearing a donkey skin. She wanted the king to find her. After searching for many months, the king saw her and immediately recognised her.

Then, the princess married the king.

JUNE 5

Samantha and Sienna

Samantha and Sienna were mischievous Mermaids. Their father often warned them, 'Do not venture into the dark caves under the sea.'

But the Mermaids were too playful to listen.

One day, Samantha challenged Sienna to go into the dark caves. Sienna accepted and swam deep into the sea. There, she saw green creatures with a yellow mane and tail.

The green creatures caught Sienna and dragged her into the caves.

Meanwhile, frightened Samantha confessed everything to her father. He went to the dark caves with other Mermen and Sienna was rescued.

From then, the Mermaids always listened to their father.

JUNE 6

The Cinnamon Bird

A long time ago, the Cinnamon Bird went to the Fairy Queen for help. She said, 'As you know, I make my nest at the top of a Cinnamon tree. That is how I got my name, too.'

The Fairy Queen asked, 'But what is the problem, my dear?'

The Cinnamon Bird said, 'People who want Cinnamon sticks throw stones at the tree and thus hurt my nest.'

The Fairy Tree advised, 'From now on, I grant that you live on Cinnamon trees that are very far from humans.'

The Cinnamon Bird was happy and thanked the Fairy Queen.

JUNE 7

The Goblins love for Children

Once, there lived a Woodcutter family at the edge of a thick forest. The Woodcutter had two little children who lived with their Grandparents in a town. In summer, the children visited their parents.

One night, the Woodcutter was woken up by strange noises. He saw small men with thick hair and beards going out of the window.

The next morning, the children found small gifts near their beds. The Woodcutter's wife said, 'The little men must have been Goblins. They love children and come to give them presents.'

The children were very happy and thanked the Goblins aloud.

JUNE 8

Wren, the Little Pixie

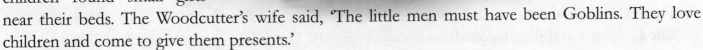

Once, there lived a little Pixie named Wren. Wren did not like being a Pixie. He complained, 'I hate being so short. I don't like my pointed ears and upturned nose.'

During a Fairy Festival, Wren went up to the Fairy Godmother and said, 'Please grant me a wish. I want to be tall.'

Fairy Godmother explained, 'Wren, Pixies are kind and helpful folk. Children all over the world love Pixies as they help Santa Claus in making toys for Christmas.'

Wren understood how important Pixies were to the world. From then on, he never complained about being a Pixie.

JUNE 9

The Dolphins and the Fishermen

Once, some Fishermen were fishing in the sea. They saw a family of Dolphins swimming nearby. The Dolphins were actually guarding three Mermaid sisters.

Then, one Fisherman said, 'Look, there are three Mermaids with the Dolphins!'

A young Dolphin thought, 'These Fishermen are sure to catch the Mermaid sisters.'

So, before the Fishermen could throw their nets at the Mermaid sisters, the Dolphin dived down and simply pushed the boat a little.

The Fishermen lost their balance and fell into the sea, getting very wet!

The Dolphins and the Mermaids swam away quickly. Thus, the Dolphins saved their friends.

JUNE 10

An Elf named Joey

Once, there was a little Elf named Joey. When the Elf Mother read stories to Elf children, they laughed at happy endings and cried at sad endings. But everyone teased Joey because he never laughed or cried at anything.

One day, Joey said to the Elf Mother, 'Please help me!'

She said, 'Wear this Golden Crown. You will feel all emotions like happiness, sadness and gratitude.'

So, Joey wore the Crown.

When the Elf Mother read a sad story that day, Joey started weeping. His friends were surprised. They felt sad to see him cry, and never teased him again.

JUNE 11

The Fisherman

Once upon a time, there was a brave Fisherman.

One day, he caught a very big fish in his net. When he looked closer, he saw that it was a Mermaid!

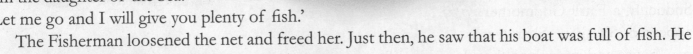

The tail of the Mermaid was of a beautiful green colour. The Fisherman was amazed. He said, 'Who are you?'

The Mermaid replied, 'I am the daughter of the Sea. Let me go and I will give you plenty of fish.'

The Fisherman loosened the net and freed her. Just then, he saw that his boat was full of fish. He went home happy and grateful.

JUNE 12

The Mighty Dragon

Once upon a time, there was a beautiful Princess. She had a pet Dragon. He was tame and friendly, but everyone was afraid of him.

One day, an Evil Dragon attacked the village. The Princess wanted to help her people. She led the army to fight it. However, the Evil Dragon was too strong and defeated them.

Suddenly, the Princess's Dragon flew up into the sky. He was brave and strong, and fought the Evil Dragon for hours. Finally, the Princess's Dragon defeated the Evil Dragon.

Everybody thanked him and became his friend. They were no longer afraid of him.

JUNE 13

The Fairy Godmother

Once upon a time, there was a girl named Sharon. Her family was very poor. She worked hard to feed her brothers and sisters.

One day, while coming back from work Sharon saw a little rabbit. The rabbit had a message around its neck. She read it, 'If you make a wish upon a star, then it will come true.'

That night, Sharon saw a shooting star. She made a wish. Suddenly, a Fairy Godmother appeared. She gave Sharon a new house and everything that she wished for.

Sharon was very happy and thankful, and lived happily ever after.

JUNE 14

The Friendly Ogre

Long ago, there lived a friendly Ogre. However, everyone in the village was afraid of him. He was big and people became frightened because of his height.

One day, there was an earthquake. The village school was shaking and was going to fall down. Just then, the Ogre came and held up the roof of the school. The school children were able to run to safety and no one was hurt.

Everyone thanked the friendly Ogre and apologised for their behaviour. They realised that the Ogre just wanted to help them.

Everyone became the Ogre's friend and he was happy.

JUNE 15

Kay and Mary

Long ago, a brother named Kay lived with his sister Mary. Kay was very naughty and never listened to his sister.

One day, Kay went into the Owl City and was lost. An Evil Witch captured him and tied him to a tree.

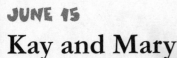

Mary went searching for her brother and saw him tied to the tree. She was very intelligent. She gathered up wood and lit a fire. When the Witch saw the smoke she came running towards it. When she got close, Mary pushed her into the fire.

Thus, Mary saved her brother and they went back home to their mother.

JUNE 16

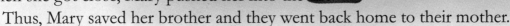

The Magic Money-Bag

Once, a kind young man lived in a village. Everyone called him 'Mango-Eater' as he ate only mangoes. He made everyone laugh and everybody liked him.

One day, Mango-Eater found an old purse. On the back of the purse, was embroidered, 'Ask and you shall get it.' It was a magic money-bag!

Mango-Eater asked for a small amount of money. Surprisingly, the same amount of money magically appeared in the money-bag.

Now, Mango-Eater asked for a little money every day and became rich. However, he was a noble man. So, he used most of this money to help needy people.

JUNE 17

The Donkey-Prince

A long time ago, a King accidentally killed an Old Man. Seeing this, the Old Man's Wife cursed the King, 'Your son shall be born in the skin of an animal.'

Soon, the Queen gave birth to a Donkey. However, the Donkey grew up to become a great musician.

One day, while the Donkey sat playing at his window, a Flower-Girl heard his song. She was touched by his music and fell in love with him. Soon, they were married.

As time passed, the Flower-Girl's love removed the Donkey Prince's curse and he was transformed into a handsome man.

JUNE 18

The Adopted Elf

A poor Hunter did not have any children. He and his Wife really wanted a child.

One day, they saw an Elf in their garden and adopted it. The Hunter and his Wife loved the little Elf deeply. They took great care of him.

One day, a Circus-Master saw this Elf and wanted to buy him. The Hunter and his Wife refused to sell their son. So, the Circus-Master stole him. This made the Elf angry. He punished the Circus Master by releasing all the animals in his circus.

Then, the Elf ran away and returned home to his parents!

JUNE 19

The Magical Horse

Once, a Farmer had a magical Horse. Whenever he said 'Abracadabra', the Horse would spit out gold coins. The Farmer became quite rich.

One day, the Farmer went to a hotel. To pay the bill, he went out to the Horse to get some coins. However, the Hotel-Keeper followed him and discovered his secret.

Now, he told the Farmer, 'Tell your horse to give me one thousand gold coins.'

The Farmer said 'Abracadabra' but the Horse did not spit a single gold coin.

Finally, the greedy Hotel-Keeper thought he had made a mistake, and let the Horse and Farmer go.

JUNE 20

The Princess' Voice

Once, a young Princess lost her voice. She now spent all day in the garden taking care of flowers. The Queen of flowers was delighted with her work. So, she made a plan to return her voice.

One day, a blue flower appeared in the garden. At once, the Princess fell in love with its colour. However, the King plucked the blue flower.

Shocked by her father's behaviour, the Princess shouted, 'Father, flowers too have a life like us.'

Hearing her voice, the King was delighted. From that day, he never let anyone harm any plant in his kingdom.

JUNE 21

The Bewitched Girl

In a faraway land, a young Soldier saw a fire in the woods. Amidst the flames, he saw a young Girl crying for help. She shouted, 'Save me!'

The Soldier jumped into the fire and pulled her out of the flames. They fell in love and he wanted to marry her

The Girl thanked him, but said, 'You will have to wait for five years, as I am cursed and cannot marry till then.'

The young Soldier loved her very much, so he waited till her curse was over. Then, they married and went to the land of fairies.

JUNE 22

The Wise Rabbit

Once, a Rabbit wanted to become wise. So, he went to a Witch and pleaded to make him wise. She said, 'I need Python's poison to make the wisdom potion.'

So, the smart Rabbit went to the Python's lair and said, 'Python, a huge log has been found. They say it's even longer than you. You must prove them wrong.'

Hearing this, the proud Python came out and stretched out on the log. The Rabbit quickly tied him to the log and took him to the Witch.

Now, the Witch took the Python's poison and made Rabbit the wisest animal.

JUNE 23

The Trapped Genie

Long ago, a young Boy was walking in a forest. He heard a voice, 'Please help me!'

He looked around and saw a small bottle lying on the ground. He picked it up and saw a little Man in it yelling, 'Please open the cork.'

The Boy opened the cork. The Man came out and grew in size, accompanied by a lot of smoke.

He said, 'I'm a Genie. As you saved me, I'll reward you. Take this magic dagger. Anything you touch with it will turn to gold.'

The Boy took the dagger and soon became rich.

JUNE 24

The Officer's Locket

One day, an Officer followed some thieves into the forest. Unfortunately, they got away. Tired by the chase, he went to the river. As he bent down to drink water, his locket slipped from his neck and fell into the water.

The River Fairy appeared and said, 'Don't worry. I'll get your locket.'

She dived into the river and came out with a golden, silver and a bronze locket. She asked him, 'Which one of this is yours?'

The Officer picked up the bronze locket. Pleased with the Officer's honesty, the Sea Fairy gave him all the three lockets!

JUNE 25

Chubby Manny

Once, a chubby little boy named Manny lived in a village.

One day, a Witch saw him. She thought, 'This boy will make a good meal for me.'

She disguised herself and went to Manny with some presents. When Manny went near the Witch, she put him in her sack.

On reaching home, the Witch lit the fire to cook Manny. However, she had forgotten her big pan in the sack.

As soon as she opened the sack, Manny hit her with the pan! He jumped out and rushed back home. He never went near strangers again.

JUNE 26

The Princess and the Frog

Once, a Princess lost her ball in a lake. As she started crying, a Frog leapt out of the water and brought back her ball. From that day on, they became fast friends.

Every day, the Princess and the Frog played near the lake. The Frog taught the Princess to swim. Eventually, they fell in love.

However, the Princess knew that they could not get married. So, she went to the Sea-Fairy and requested, 'Turn me into a Frog so that I can live in the water.'

The Sea-Fairy agreed. And, the two Frog lived happily in the lake.

JUNE 27

The Magic Violin

Once, a Violinist had a magic violin. The music that came out of the violin could control everybody.

One day, while the Violinist was crossing a forest, a Bear tried to attack him. The Violinist quickly took out his violin and played a beautiful tune. Hearing the music, the Bear stood still.

The Violinist told him to stop attacking people. The Bear promised to do so. He said, 'Please teach me this beautiful music.'

So, the Violinist taught the Bear music. Since then, the animals of the forest loved to listen to the Bear, and he never attacked anyone again.

JUNE 28

The Thirsty Man

Once, a Thirsty Man wandered in the woods. Soon, he found a well. The Man sat in one of the buckets and went to the bottom of the well to drink water.

However, as he tried to go up, he realised there was no one to pull him out of the well. He prayed to God for help.

Just then, God sent down one of his Angels. The Angel waved her hand and the water began to rise up. Soon, the water reached the top of the well and the Man jumped out.

He thanked God for helping him.

JUNE 29

The Snail's Wedding

An Old Snail couple lived with their Son in the woods. They were a happy family except for one problem. They wanted to find a bride for their Son. However, since no other snails lived in this forest, they could not find a match.

One day, the Queen of Butterflies dropped a beautiful Female Snail in the Old Couple's garden. The Couple liked the Female Snail very much and married her to their Son.

The Ants became the bridesmaids, the Fireflies took care of the lightening arrangement and the Crickets organised the orchestra. It was a beautiful wedding indeed!

JUNE 30

The Honest Porter

Once, there lived a poor Porter. He went to a nearby village to earn a living.

One afternoon while going to work, the Potter's tools fell into a puddle. He became very sad.

Just then, the Forest Nymph appeared. She asked, 'What's the matter, my friend?'

The Porter told her what had happened. She showed him a gold tool and asked if it was his. He said that it wasn't.

The Forest Nymph rewarded the Porter for his honesty. She said, 'As long as you remain honest, you will be happy and rich.'

The Porter thanked her, and stayed honest.

JULY 1

The Lost Nymph

One day, a young Water-Nymph wandered far away from home. Finding herself alone, she became very scared and started crying.

A wicked Whale saw her and thought, 'I must kidnap and eat her.'

Thinking so, the Whale went to the Nymph and said, 'I'll take you back home. I am familiar with the entire ocean.'

The Nymph agreed and sat on the Whale's back. On the way, the Nymph began to sing.

Luckily, her friends heard her voice and followed it. Soon, they reached her and took her away from the Whale. Thus, her friends saved her life.

JULY 2

The Fisherman and his Wife

A Fisherman and his Wife lived in a hut.

One day, the Fisherman caught a Golden Fish. It requested, 'Please let me go. I am an Enchanted Prince.

The Fisherman let the Fish go. But his Wife said, 'Ask it for a nice house.'

So, the Fisherman went back and the Golden Fish granted the wish.

However, the greedy Wife wanted more. She got a castle, became Queen, then an Empress.

Then, the Wife wished to become God. The Fish said, 'Your greed keeps increasing. So you will get nothing!'

Sure enough, they were left with just their old hut.

JULY 3

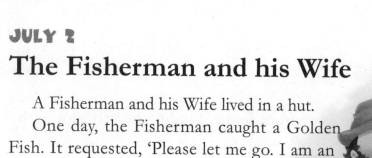

The Pixie and the Little Girl

Once, an ugly Pixie lived in a wood.

Whenever the Pixie went to the village, people ran away saying, 'You are so ugly. We can't be friends with you.'

The sad Pixie thought, 'I will give half my magical powers to anyone who will become my friend.'

The next day, the Pixie met a little Girl. She saw him and began to play with him. Seeing this, the Pixie asked, 'Don't you find me ugly?'

She replied, 'Only the beauty of friends' hearts matter.'

The Pixie was happy and gave half his magical powers to her. After this, they remained friends forever.

JULY 4

The Twelve Dancing Princesses

A king had twelve daughters. They slept in a locked room, but every morning, their shoes were worn out.

The king announced, 'Whoever finds out the truth can marry one of the princesses.'

A soldier offered to try. He had a magical cloak, which made him invisible.

That night, he followed the princesses when they went through a trap door to an enchanted land. They danced all night. The soldier took some golden leaves from there. He also took one of the princesses' gloves as a proof.

He told the king everything. He married the eldest princess and lived happily.

JULY 5

The Golden Eagle

Chichinatsu was the greatest emperor of Japan. He defeated all his enemies and ruled fairly.

One day, when he had grown old and was sitting in the park, Chichinatsu saw a golden eagle in the sky. The eagle landed at his feet.

Chichinatsu understood the sign. He asked, 'Is it my time to leave this world?'

The eagle nodded. Without delay, Chichinatsu bade farewell to his family and friends.

The eagle then took him to heaven. The Japanese people mourned his death for many years as they had never been as rich and happy as they were under his rule.

JULY 6

The Piggy-Bank

The Piggy-Bank in Ronny's room was full of coins. It was so full that it didn't even rattle when shaken. All the other toys respected it because of its wealth. However, it wasn't proud and loved all the toys.

One day, Ronny tried to push another coin into the Piggy-Bank. But it was so full that it shattered into pieces.

The toys were sad as they had lost their friend. Seeing them unhappy, a Fairy came to the playroom at night. Using a magic spell, she fixed the Piggy-Bank. All the toys thanked her. The Piggy-Bank was also very grateful.

JULY 7

The Magic Fish-Bone

A poor man lived in a village. He could not provide his family with enough food.

Pitying the family's condition, the sea-fairy came to his daughter, Alice.

She gave her a large salmon and said, 'Do not throw the bone as it's magical. It will grant you one wish.'

After some time, Alice's father's health condition worsened. The entire family was worried.

Now, Alice took out the fish-bone to use a wish. The sea-fairy appeared and crushed the bone. Alice threw the bone powder from a cliff wishing for her father's health.

He was healed and Alice thanked the sea-fairy.

JULY 8

The Cruel Lion

Long ago, a cruel lion lived in a forest. He killed animals for fun. All the animals were scared of him.

One day, the animals decided to go to the magical dragon on the hill top. They met the dragon and requested, 'Dragon, our king, the lion, is very cruel. Please help us.'

The dragon agreed and went to the forest with them.

Then, a strange thing happened. The magical dragon merely looked at the lion and the lion was burnt to ashes! The whole forest was happy. They thanked the dragon and made him their new king.

JULY 9

How the Sun Came To Be

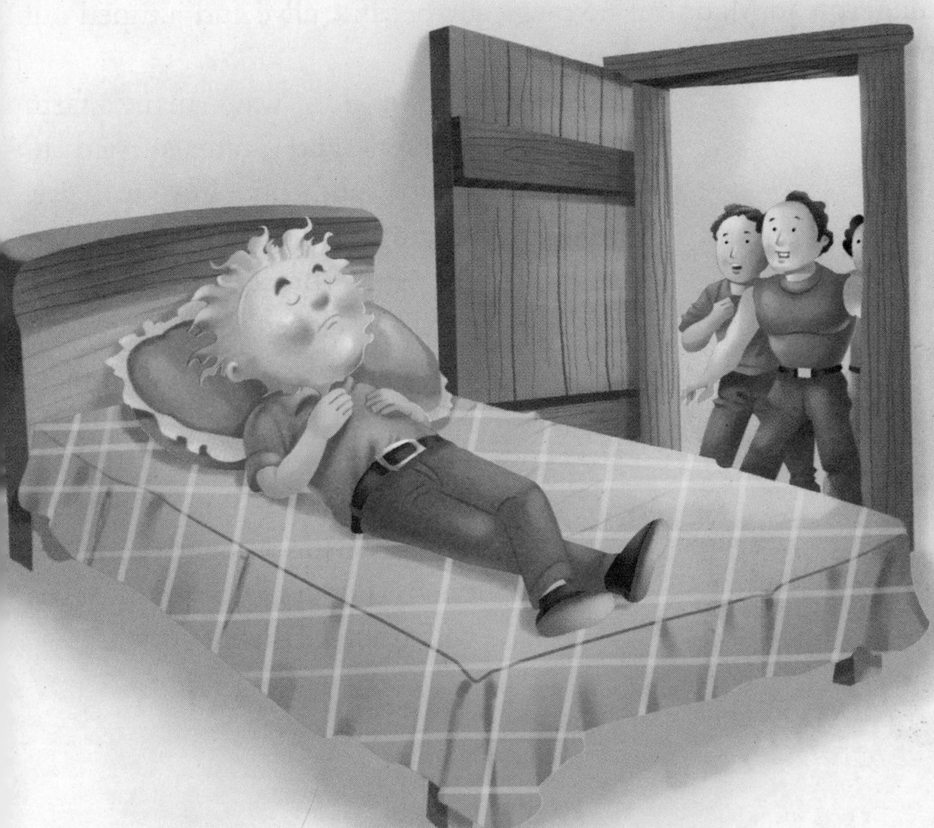

In ancient times, the Sun used to be a man. He was very lazy and slept all day. So, the Earth was always dark and cold.

The distressed people decided to do something about the situation. They sent the strongest men to go deal with the Sun.

When the men reached the Sun's home, they saw that he was sleeping as usual. They grabbed him by the arms and feet and threw him into the sky.

The Sun flew at such a high speed that he turned into a round ball. Ever since then, he has been revolving around Earth.

JULY 10

The Woman's Gold Beans

Long ago, a Foolish Woman had a bag of gold beans. They were magical and multiplied every day.

One day, a Pot-Seller came and offered her a golden pot. She thought, 'This golden pot looks more expensive than my beans. I shall exchange it for them.'

So, the Woman gave away her magical golden beans and took the pot. The next day, she tried to sell the pot for more coins. Sadly, she realised that the pot was not really made of gold! The Pot-Seller had lied to her.

She realised her foolishness but it was too late.

JULY 11

The Gingerbread Man

An Old Woman once baked a Gingerbread Man. But he magically became alive and jumped out from her oven. The Woman tried to catch him but he ran away.

On his way, many farm workers and animals tried to catch him, but he ran away singing, 'You can't catch me, I'm the Gingerbread Man.'

The clever Fox saw him and wanted to eat him. So he pretended to be a friend. As soon as the Gingerbread Man came closer, the Fox ate him up. The poor silly Gingerbread Man cried, 'I'm quarter gone.... I'm half gone... I'm all gone!'

JULY 12

The Knight and his Dragon

Once, a Knight had a beautiful flying Dragon. The Knight wanted to get married, but could not find the right bride.

So, he finally said to the Dragon, 'Take me to the land where I can find my love.'

The Dragon was excited to help his master. The Dragon took him to a beautiful castle. There, the Knight saw a beautiful Princess dressed in a sparkling gown. As soon as the Knight and the Princess saw each other, they fell in love.

Then, they both got married and lived happily ever after, taking good care of the Dragon.

JULY 13

The Magic Pen

Once, a Student was walking in the woods. Suddenly, a strange Woman approached him. She said, 'If you catch a swarm of bees for me, I'll reward you with something extraordinary.'

The Student was very smart. He opened a pumpkin and put it near a bee-hive. When the bees entered the pumpkin, the Student closed the pumpkin and took it to the Woman.

The Woman was amazed at the Student's smartness. She gave him a magic pen. The pen helped to complete the Student's home work and exam papers. With its help, he always came first in the class.

JULY 14

The Sorceress and the King

Once, a handsome young King ruled a large kingdom. A Sorceress wanted to marry him.

However, the King did not like her and refused. He wanted to marry a beautiful Fairy. This made the Sorceress very angry. She decided to cast a spell and make him fall in love with her.

But before she could do this, the Fairy found out about it. The Fairy put a shield around the King, so that no spells could affect him. When the Sorceress realised this, she went away. The Fairy then married the King, and they lived together very happily.

JULY 15

The Sea Maiden

One day, a handsome man, Imam, lay on the beach. Suddenly, a magical Seagull landed there. She fell in love with Imam.

The Seagull magically transformed herself into a young Maiden and dived into the ocean. Imam thought that she was about to drown and rescued her.

Now, the Maiden thanked Imam and said, 'Come to my father's kingdom. He'll reward you.'

Imam went with the Maiden to a hidden castle deep down the sea. There, the Sea-King welcomed him and said, 'I give you my daughter's hand in marriage.'

After this, Imam became the King of the Oceans!

JULY 16

The Magic Cow

Once, a rag-picker named Julie found a magical Cow. Whenever she had to go out, she entered one of the Cow's ears. When she came out from the other ear, she was well-dressed and well-fed.

On returning home, Julie entered one ear and on coming out from the other, she was again dressed in her rags.

One day, an Old Woman saw all this. She wanted to become young again. Thus, she stole the cow and entered its ear. Sadly, she took a wrong turn and she turned into a calf!

That is how God punished her for stealing.

JULY 17

The Fountain of Love

Once, in the dwarf land, a young female Gnome wished to marry the King Gnome. So, she proposed him to marry her.

The King Gnome said, 'If you come to me neither clothed nor naked, neither on foot nor on horse-back, neither with a gift nor without; I shall marry you.'

The next day, the female Gnome came to the palace wearing a fish-net, on the back of a rabbit and with a butterfly in her hand, which she released in front of him.

This fulfilled all the three conditions. The King Gnome admired her cleverness and married her.

JULY 18

The Golden Fish

Once, a little Golden Fish was caught in a Fisherman's net. It made a sad face and begged the Fisherman to let it go. Touched by its expression, the Fisherman put the Golden Fish back in the water. The grateful Fish said, 'As you have spared my life, I shall reward you soon.' Saying so, it swam away.

When the Fisherman reached home, he saw that his hut had transformed into a grand manor. His Wife wore rich clothes and was adorned with jewels. His children had lots of toys to play with. Thus, his kindness was well rewarded!

JULY 19

The Magic Cloak

Once, a boy named Adam found a magic cloak in his grandfather's old chest. This cloak kept Adam warm in winter days and cool in the summer days.

One day, Adam met a poor Boy. The Boy wore a cloak with many holes in it. Adam boasted, 'Your cloak is torn and ragged, but mine is magical!'

The poor Boy said, 'My cloak is magical, too. The air comes in from one hole and goes out through another.'

On hearing this, Adam realised how silly he was to boast. He apologised and gave the Boy a nice cloak without holes.

JULY 20

The Dragon of Samau Lake

Himaku was a brave knight.

One day, he was called by the King. When he reached the court, the King said, 'My kingdom is threatened by a fierce Dragon. He lives in the Samau Lake. I've heard that only you can defeat it.'

Hearing this, Himaku went to Samau Lake. Seeing him, the Dragon let out a stream of fire.

However, Himaku was not scared. He jumped on the Dragon's back and struck it with his sword. Immediately, the Dragon let out a roar and fell on the ground.

The entire kingdom thanked Himaku for saving them from the Dragon.

JULY 21

The Ugly Duckling

Once, there was a Duckling who was teased for being ugly by all the farm animals.

The sad little Duckling left home and wandered till an old woman took him in. But her cat and hen teased him and he left again.

He saw a flock of swans and thought, 'How I wish I was like them.'

Soon, winter came and a Farmer took the Duckling home. There, he was troubled by the farmer's children.

When spring came, he went to a lake. He was welcomed by some swans. He realised that he had grown up into a beautiful swan!

JULY 22

The Mice's Wedding

Naughty Harry always troubled innocent animals like mice and lizards.

One day, he was woken up by the dream-fairy. She said, 'Harry, let us go to the wedding of the mice! You will then learn to respect them.'

Then, she waved her magic wand. Immediately, they reached a tunnel.

There, a mouse was sitting in a little carriage with his bride. Cheese delicacies were laid out on the table for the guests. Soon, everybody began to dance. Harry joined them, too.

Before morning, the dream-fairy dropped Harry back to his bed. He remembered this wedding forever and never troubled animals again.

JULY 23

Furry's Revenge

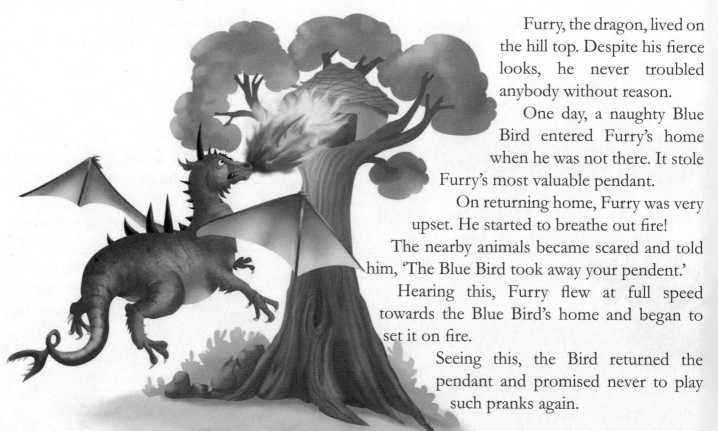

Furry, the dragon, lived on the hill top. Despite his fierce looks, he never troubled anybody without reason.

One day, a naughty Blue Bird entered Furry's home when he was not there. It stole Furry's most valuable pendant.

On returning home, Furry was very upset. He started to breathe out fire!

The nearby animals became scared and told him, 'The Blue Bird took away your pendent.'

Hearing this, Furry flew at full speed towards the Blue Bird's home and began to set it on fire.

Seeing this, the Bird returned the pendant and promised never to play such pranks again.

JULY 24

The Young Centaur

Long ago, Centaurs lived in a valley. The nearby forest was full of dangerous monsters. The Centaurs never went there.

One day, a young Centaur said to his friends, 'Anyone who spends an hour in the woods will be made our leader. I'll try first.'

His friends tried to stop him but he didn't listen. As soon as the young Centaur entered the woods, a Goblin caught him in his net.

The Centaur cried for help. Fortunately, a Squirrel saw him and cut through his net. The Centaur had learnt his lesson, and never went into the dangerous forest again.

JULY 25

The Unicorn's Birthday

Long ago, a family of Unicorns lived in a forest. On Baby Unicorn's birthday, all the animals were invited to a party. They wore lovely dresses and brought gifts for Baby Unicorn.

But Baby Unicorn was unhappy. His parents asked, 'Why do you look so sad?'

Baby Unicorn replied, 'No one brought a birthday cake for me.'

Suddenly, the big fat Elephant came with a huge cake. Now, Baby Unicorn was delighted. He cut the cake and served it to everybody.

All the guests danced and enjoyed themselves. Everyone thanked the Unicorn family for a wonderful party.

JULY 26

The Walking Snake

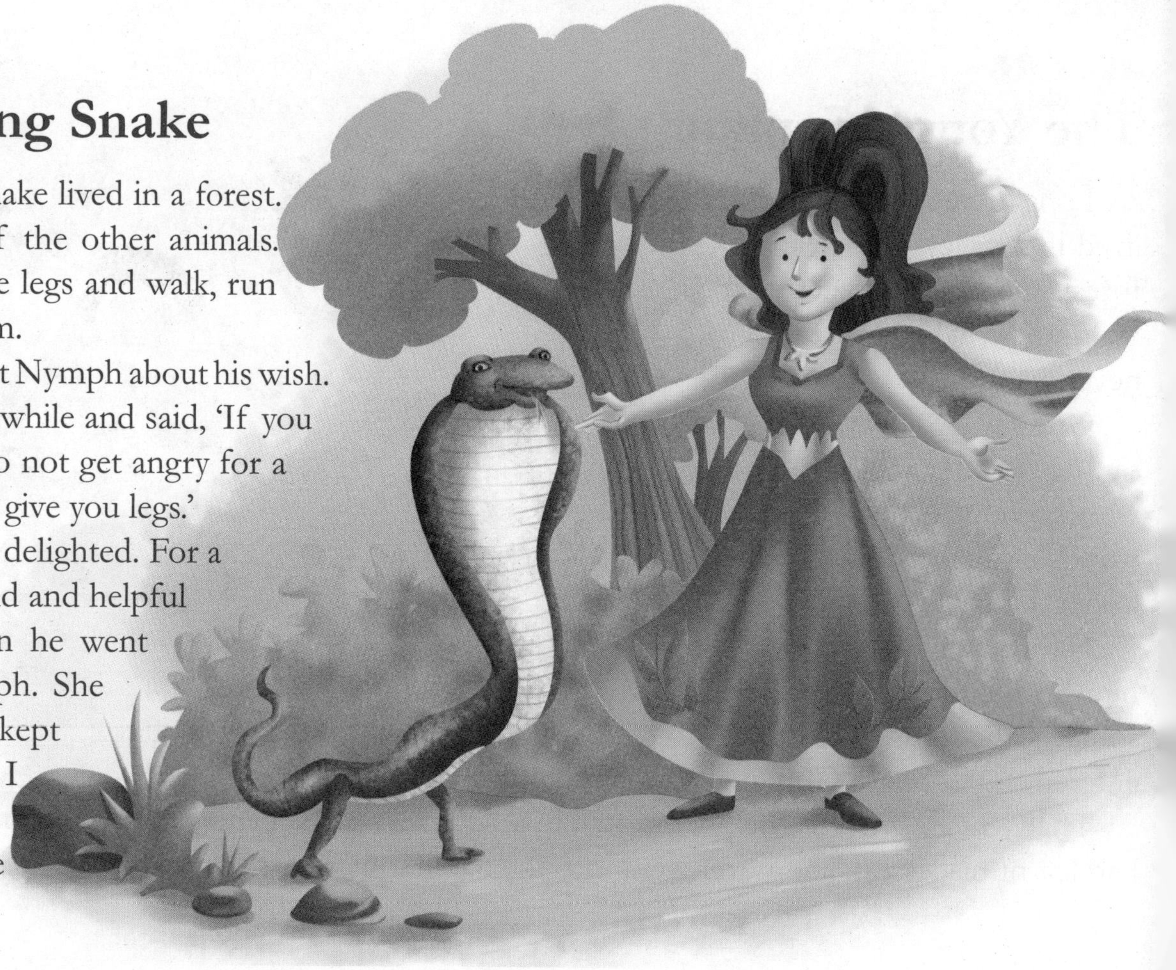

Long ago, a Snake lived in a forest. He was jealous of the other animals. He wished to have legs and walk, run and jump like them.

He told a Forest Nymph about his wish. She thought for a while and said, 'If you help others and do not get angry for a month, then I can give you legs.'

The snake was delighted. For a month, he was kind and helpful to everyone. Then he went back to the Nymph. She said, 'You have kept your promise, so I shall keep mine.'

Thus, the Snake got legs!

JULY 27

The Ogre and the Pigs

Long ago, a wise Wolf lived in a forest. He preached to the animals all day. Three lazy little Pigs were tired of this habit of his. So, they decided to get rid of him.

The Pigs went to a ferocious Ogre and said, 'We are tired of the wise Wolf. Kill him for us. He will serve as a good meal for you.'

The Ogre looked at the Pigs and thought, 'These plump Pigs will be more delicious than the Wolf.'

The Ogre quickly ate up the three Pigs, and thus they got punished for their bad thoughts.

JULY 28

The Magical Horn

A beautiful girl named Patricia lived in a village.

One day, she saw an Elf being chased by a cat. She ran to save the Elf and shooed the cat away.

The grateful Elf gave her a magical horn and said, 'Whenever you are in trouble, blow this magic horn. I'll come to help you.'

One day, a Thief broke into her house. Immediately, Patricia blew the magic horn.

In an instant, the Elf appeared. He blew a powder over the Thief which caused him to itch all over!

The Thief scratched and scratched, until the Police took him away!

JULY 29

The Magic Carpet

Long ago, a little Girl fell ill. The doctors took a long time to cure her. Her parents tried to keep her happy, but even after being cured, she remained sad.

One day, a Fairy saw the Girl's sad face and thought, 'I must make her smile.'

The Fairy went to the Girl and said, 'I have a magic carpet. It can fly you to any place you want.'

The Girl sat and the carpet flew her to toy land. Playing with her favourite toys, she laughed to her heart's content. From then on, the Girl was never sad again.

JULY 30

The Mermaid's Husband

The Sea-King had a beautiful Mermaid daughter.

One day, the Sea-King decided to marry his daughter.

The Mermaid said, 'I will marry the man who will risk his life for me.'

One day, while the Mermaid relaxed on the beach, a Sea-Dragon attacked her. Seeing this, a young Man charged at the Dragon and pierced its heart with his sword.

The Mermaid instantly fell in love with him. She took him to the Sea-King and requested, 'Make me a human so that I can live with this man on Earth.'

The Sea-King agreed and married them in a grand ceremony!

JULY 31

The Warrior's Sword

Long ago, a handsome Warrior went to a forest. There, he was attacked by goblins. Since the Warrior was strong, he fought them bravely.

Seeing his courage, the guardian Fairy of the forest fell in love with him. She decided to marry him.

However, the Warrior had to leave for a battle. So, the Fairy gave him a magical sword and said, 'This sword will ensure your victory and safe return.'

With the sword's help, the Warrior defeated his enemies and returned to the forest. Soon after, he married the Fairy and they lived happily ever after.

AUGUST 1

The Birth of Stars

In ancient times, the Sky was not beautiful. The Moon was the only source of light at night. Since the Moon could not provide enough light, the Angels thought of looking for something new.

They came down to Earth and searched for a new source. Suddenly, they came across some fireflies. They were delighted to see the little glowing lights on their back.

Thus, the Angels took these fireflies with them and stuck them in the sky. They arranged them in various patterns and shapes which are now known as Constellations.

This is how the Stars made the sky so beautiful.

AUGUST 2

The Three Tasks

Three princes went out to seek their fortune. The third prince was a simpleton. He stopped his brothers when they wanted to destroy an anthill, kill ducks and put a beehive on fire.

The brothers went to a castle where they had to complete three tasks to save three princesses from a spell. The older brothers failed the tasks.

The simpleton succeeded by collecting ten thousand pearls with the help of the ants. The ducks helped him bring a key from the lake and the queen bee helped him pick the right princess who had eaten honey.

The simpleton married her.

AUGUST 3

The Elfin Hill

Two Lizards were once talking about the arrangements going on inside the Elfin Hill. Just then, an old maid Elf hurried out and called a Raven to deliver invitations.

The Elf Princesses were practicing dancing and singing. The Elf King told his youngest daughter, 'I have arranged marriages between two of you and the two sons of the Goblin Chief.'

During the feast, the Elf daughters performed their talents. But, the Goblin sons were rude and manner-less. The youngest daughter scolded them for their behaviour and won the heart of the Goblin King. He married her and the feast ended.

AUGUST 4

The Twelve Huntsmen

A prince was in love with a maiden. But, he promised the dying king to marry a princess and was crowned the new king.

The maiden meanwhile gathered eleven maidens who looked exactly like her. Then, they dressed as huntsmen and went to court.

The king had a pet lion who said, 'Put them to test by rolling peas under their feet.'

The maiden heard this and told her companions to step firmly.

One day, when the king's fiancée came, the maiden fainted. The king saw the ring he had given her and realised how much she loved him. He married her and lived happily.

AUGUST 5

The Farmer's Bird Friends

A farmer grew red and pink tulips in his field. People from the neighbouring villages came to buy them.

The farmer often spoke to birds and they taught him about tulips.

One day, he noticed something strange. Amidst the red and pink tulips, there were grey ones. He spoke to his bird friends, 'This is quite shocking! Why did this happen?'

The birds said, 'The grey ones are pretty, too. The customers will like them.'

The farmer picked grey tulips to his shop. The customers loved them and placed large orders for them. The farmer started growing grey tulips, too.

AUGUST 6

Unicorns for the Spring Festival

Tia and Lya went to the fairy school to learn arts.

One day, the fairy-godmother said, 'Its spring festival tomorrow. Please bring a unicorn for the merry-go-round.'

Tia and Lya found two unicorns in the forest. Lya cried, while tying them, 'I wish I had paid more attention when the fairy-godmother taught us how to tie a knot.'

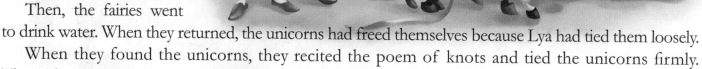

Then, the fairies went to drink water. When they returned, the unicorns had freed themselves because Lya had tied them loosely.

When they found the unicorns, they recited the poem of knots and tied the unicorns firmly. Then, they went to the spring festival.

AUGUST 7

Innocent Yendo

Yendo was a kind and loving man. However, someone spread rumours about him. As a result, he was thrown into jail.

There, Yendo prayed hard for get justice. So, the Goddess of Justice came to him. She gave him a pair of magical wings and said, 'Stick them to your back using wax.'

Yendo gathered wax for days. Then, he attached the wings to his back and flew out of the prison.

The King's guards saw him and were amazed. However, before anybody could catch him, Yendo flew to faraway land. He thanked the Goddess of Justice for saving his life.

AUGUST 8

Comac, the Courageous

Comac was a skilled and valiant warrior. Many monsters died at his hands.

Once upon a time, his town was attacked by a large and ferocious Minotaur. Minotaur was a savage beast. It ate people alive.

The King sent Comac to battle with the beast. Seeing him, Minotaur mocked, 'You are a mere human. You can't defeat me.'

Saying so, Minotaur leapt at Comac. Comac dodged him and ran straight into the Minotaur with his sword. He dug his sword deep into Minotaur's heart.

Within minutes, Minotaur fell on the ground and died. Everyone thanked and praised Comac for his bravery.

AUGUST 9

The Tailor Elves

Once, an old Elf couple lived in a small town.

One day, they saw poor children without warm clothes. The Wife said, 'Dear husband, during winter many of these children will die of cold. We must help them.'

The Husband agreed. So, the couple went to the dump yard and collected old woollen clothes. Then, they set to work, cutting, knitting and pasting together. In a week, they had made clothes for all the children.

At night, the Elf couple left these clothes by the poor children's bedsides. All the children were happy to see such wonderful clothes.

AUGUST 10

The Wolf and the Girl

Once, a Wolf was wandering in the woods in search of food. Suddenly, he saw a cottage in a clearing. A young Girl was sitting outside the cottage. She was feeding the birds and singing to them.

The Wolf was mesmerised by her voice and beauty and fell in love with her.

So, he went to his friend, the Goblin to ask for help. The Goblin said, 'Drink this magic potion. It will turn you into a handsome young Man.'

The Wolf happily drank the potion and transformed into a Man. Then, he married the Girl and lived happily with her.

AUGUST 11

The Troll

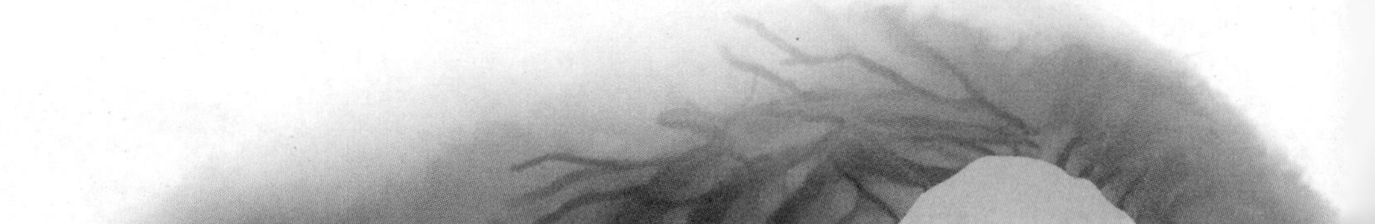

Hachi was a young magician who roamed the forests. His Mother often warned him, 'Do not go to the forest alone. You might bump into a dangerous creature.'

However, Hachi never listened and went to the forest every day.

One day, while coming back home from the forest, Hachi lost his way. After wandering for a while, he reached a cave. To his horror, a Troll came out of the cave and grabbed him.

Immediately, Hachi waved his wand and cast a spell at the Troll. He dropped Hachi and fell down.

Now, Hachi ran quickly and saved his life.

AUGUST 12

The Rainbow

Long ago, on a rainy day, Victor heard a loud shriek. A little Elf was caught by a big fat Cat.

At once, Victor threw a stone on the cat and rescued the Elf. Then, he took the terrified Elf home.

When the Elf felt better he said, 'Friend, I am very thankful to you. As soon as the rain will end, a rainbow will be formed. Travel to its other end.'

Next morning, Victor travelled to the other side of the rainbow. To his amazement, he found a pot of gold. He took it home and lived happily forever.

AUGUST 13

Unicorn Horn

Long ago, people valued a unicorn's horn. They hunted these poor animals for horns.

Nihua was a young unicorn. His father was killed for his horn. So, Nihua lived with his mother and brothers. He wanted to protect his brothers from the hunters. However, he knew that this could not be done sitting at home.

So, Nihua organised a huge army. Then, he attacked the hunters on the edge of the forest. The hunters were terrified with the attack. They realised that the unicorns had come to take revenge. So, they ran for life and never returned to Nihua's forest.

AUGUST 14

The Gold Mortar

Once, a poor Farmer went to the King to ask for help. The King gave him a piece of land to grow crops.

While ploughing, he found a gold mortar. Being an honest man, he decided to take it to the King.

A wicked Spirit stopped him and said, 'If you take it to the King you will be left poor again.'

However, the Farmer paid no heed to its words and gave the gold mortar to the King.

Seeing the Farmer's honesty, the King was impressed. He gave the gold mortar back to him. The Farmer thanked the King and came back.

AUGUST 15

The Wooden Cow

Once, a poor Man lived alone in a town. He owned nothing except a Cow. Eventually, the Cow grew old and died.

The Man was very upset with the Cow's death. As he missed his Cow, he made a wooden Cow.

Now, he began to take care of the wooden Cow as he did of the real one. He talked to it all day. Sometimes, he even took the wooden Cow to graze in the fields.

Seeing his love for the Cow, an Angel transformed the wooden Cow into a real Cow.

Seeing the real Cow, the Man was overjoyed.

AUGUST 16

The Little Pixie

Once, a little Pixie went to a Farmer's cottage and ate his food. Then, he went to the stable, lay down on a stack of hay and fell asleep. When he woke up, he found himself in the stomach of a Horse.

The Pixie was scared and began to yell. The Farmer heard this and thought, 'Certainly my horse is possessed by some wicked spirit. I must kill it.'

Thus, the farmer killed the horse and cut it open to feed its meat to dogs. As soon as its stomach was cut open, the Pixie jumped out and ran away.

AUGUST 17

The Princess' Groom

Once, a beautiful Princess lived in a high tower. This tower had ten magical windows. The Princess could see anywhere in the world through these windows.

Many young men came to ask for her hand. However, she could see their real nature from the windows and rejected them all.

One day, a new Suitor came and proposed marriage to the Princess. Finding no fault with him, she decided to marry him.

They married and threw a grand party. All the world's kings and queens were called to attend this event.

They lived happily together in the tower and ruled righteously.

AUGUST 18

Blanch and Rosalinda

Blanch and Rosalinda lived in a small cottage with a fruit garden.

One day, a fairy came disguised as an old woman. Blanch gave her apples with ill will.

Rosalinda presented eggs with a smile. The fairy blessed, 'Blanch will be a queen and Rosalinda will have a big farm.'

Soon, a king married Blanch; while Rosalinda married a farmer's son.

Blanch was sad as a queen as everyone there taunted her as she was a commoner.

The fairy said, 'I wanted to teach you a lesson for your arrogance.'

Blanch returned to the farm and spent a life of contentment with Rosalinda.

AUGUST 19

The Clever Magician

Once, a Magician wanted to marry a Princess. However, the Princess was very arrogant and rejected him. He said to her, 'Let's play a game of hide-and-seek. If you are unable to find me, you'll have to marry me. But if you find me, I shall go away.'

The Princess agreed to his condition. The Magician went to a crow's nest and transformed himself into an egg. The Princess looked for him everywhere but could not find him.

Accepting her defeat, she called him. The Magician told her where he had been hiding. Impressed with his skill, the Princess married him.

AUGUST 20

The Sea-Nymph's Dilemma

Once upon a time, a young Sea-Nymph met with an accident. When she woke up, her face was all black and bruised. She was heart-broken to see her beautiful face in such a terrible condition.

She went to the Sea-Queen and pleaded with her for help. The Sea-Queen said, 'Bring me ten sea shells to become pretty again.'

The Sea-Nymph went to the farthest corners of the sea to search for shells. Then, she took them to the Sea-Queen.

The Sea-Queen applied the paste found in the shells on the Sea-Nymph's face. Magically, her face healed and she was beautiful again.

AUGUST 21

Mr. Sun's Illness

One day, Mr. Sun caught fever. So, he decided to take a day off. He went home, snuggled under a blanket and fell fast asleep.

However, Mr. Sun went into deep sleep and did not come out for almost a week. Everyone was worried and sent Mr. Moon to check on him.

Seeing Mr. Sun's high fever, Mr. Moon called Dr. Rainbow. Dr. Rainbow checked his temperature and gave him multi-coloured tablets to eat.

In five days' time, Mr. Sun was well again. He thanked Dr. Rainbow for his help and went back to work. Everyone was happy to see him.

AUGUST 22

The Branch of Gold

Once upon a time, there was a magical Tree in a far-off forest. It was believed that its golden branches could heal all diseases.

People brought their sick friends to the Tree and pressed a branch to the sick person's chest. The branch worked magically and healed them.

One day, a wicked Witch heard of this magical Tree. She hired a Woodcutter and said, 'Go and bring that magical Tree to me.'

So, the Woodcutter cut the Tree. Sadly, when the Witch tested its magical properties, they had vanished. The cutting of the Tree had made it lose its magic.

AUGUST 23

Serena and the Fairy

Serena was a wonderful girl but sadly, she could not walk without crutches.

One day, Serena saw her neighbour's Puppy stuck on the roof. She thought, 'I must save this Puppy or he will fall off the roof.'

So, Serena gathered courage and climbed up the roof to reach the Puppy. She fell many times but would get up again.

Finally, Serena reached the Puppy and saved him. Lo! He turned into a Fairy and said, 'I was just testing you. Pleased with your kindness and courage, I shall heal our legs.' Serena was elated for she could now run, jump and play.

AUGUST 24

The Magical Staff

A young boy wished to become the strongest in the world. So, he prayed day and night.

One day, God sent his Angel to the boy, who asked, 'What do you want?' The boy replied, 'I want to become the strongest person on earth.'

The Angel gave him a magic staff and said, 'This staff will fulfil all your wishes.'

The boy was very happy. Using his staff, he made the whole earth beautiful. He brought peace amongst all.

Also, he gave food, shelter and clothing to the poor. God was extremely pleased with him and made him an Angel.

AUGUST 25

The Flower-Fairies

Once, Flower-Fairies lived in sunflowers of a garden. However, their Gardener was very lazy. He didn't water the plants or tend to their needs.

Seeing their homes dying, the Flower-Fairies became very upset. They went to the Bees and requested them for help. The Bees replied, 'If we help you, you will have to give us nectar from the flowers.'

The Flower- Fairies agreed. So, the Bees went to the Gardener and started stinging him. They said, 'We won't stop stinging you until you water the plants regularly.'

The Gardener realised his mistake. After this, he never forgot his duties.

AUGUST 26

The Naughty Pixie

Once upon a time, there was a very naughty Pixie, who lived in the woods. He liked to play pranks on everyone he met.

One day, he saw a new Creature in the forest. As he looked very odd and peculiar, the Pixie started laughing at him. Then, he went and kicked the Creature.

Now, the Creature was a magical being. He put a curse on the Pixie and said, 'Every time you irritate someone, your stomach will start tickling.'

After this, every time the Pixie played a prank on anyone, his stomach started tickling. Thus, he stopped troubling others.

AUGUST 27

The Dishonest Shopkeeper

Once, a dishonest Shopkeeper arrived at Paradise. During his life, he had cheated many customers. The Angels didn't let him enter Paradise. However, he pleaded to them till they allowed him entry inside Paradise.

Now, the Shopkeeper mistook the Angel's kindness and thought that his own sins were not big. Also, he began to judge other people's sins.

One day, when he was looking down on Earth, he saw a Boy stealing an orange from a tree. He was about to hurl something at the Boy to punish him. Just then, an Angel stopped him and threw him out of Paradise forever.

AUGUST 28

The Dead Girl

Jack was the King's cook. His sister was dead. Whenever he felt sad, he would talk to her photo.

One day, a Courtier heard Jack talk to his sister. He looked through the peephole and only saw the Girl's life-like face. When the King heard about it, he too wanted to see the Girl's face.

Seeing the photo, the King was completely smitten by the Girl's beauty. Seeing the King's and Jack's love for the Girl, the Angels sent her back to Earth.

Jack was delighted to have his sister back. The King married her and made her his queen.

AUGUST 29

The Card-Player

Once, a Man loved playing cards. Many people lost their precious things to him as he won each game. They complained about him to Death-God.

Death-God went to bring the Man to his abode. He said, 'I'll come with you but first let us play cards.'

The Death-God agreed. However, he lost each game and the Man won.

Tired of losing, the Death-God asked, 'What will you take in return of letting me win one game.'

The Man replied, 'I shall let you win if you spare my life.'

The Death-God agreed. He won a game and went back.

AUGUST 30

Mauris, the Giant

Once, there lived a miserly Couple. Mauris, a young giant, worked hard for them. Yet, when it was time to pay him, they didn't want to give anything. Thus, they devised a plan to kill him.

So, the Couple sent Mauris down the well. When he reached the bottom, the Couple rolled a grindstone into the well to crush Mauris.

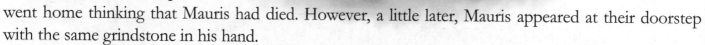

After this, the Couple went home thinking that Mauris had died. However, a little later, Mauris appeared at their doorstep with the same grindstone in his hand.

This scared the Couple. They begged for forgiveness and gave Mauris his money.

AUGUST 31

Dumbhead and the Gnome

Once, a Couple had a young Son. They cursed him all the time and called him 'Dumbhead'.

One day, they sent Dumbhead to cut wood. His Mother gave him a single slice of bread and a small water-bottle. When Dumbhead was tired, he sat down to eat. Suddenly, a Gnome appeared and said, 'I'm very hungry. Please give me something to eat.'

Dumbhead took pity and shared his meagre food with the Gnome.

Pleased by this gesture, the Gnome gave him two bags full of gold coins. Seeing the gold, the Couple felt proud of their son and stopped cursing him.

SEPTEMBER 1

King Thrushbeard

A proud Princess always found faults in every suitor who came to marry her.

One day, a King came to seek her hand. The Princess teased, 'With your crooked chin, Thrushbeard would be an apt name for you!'

The offended King disguised as a common man came back. The Princess's father was tired of her tantrums and married her to the common man.

The Princess was forced to live in a hut and work in a nearby palace. She learnt to become humble and kind.

Finally, King Thrushbeard revealed his true self and the humble Princess lived happily with him.

SEPTEMBER 2

The Green Tree Goblins

Thomas was very unhappy in the city. So, he started living in a hut in a forest.

Thomas cut the branches of a tree and said aloud, 'These branches are taking too much space!'

This upset the Green Goblins.

One night, while Thomas lay in his bed, the Green Goblins started pulling his toes. They said, 'This man is taking a lot of space. Let us throw him in the well so that we can be comfortable.'

Thomas jumped and ran far away from the forest, promising never to hurt any tree.

The Goblins and trees laughed and let him go.

SEPTEMBER 3

The Cat and the Mouse

Once, a Cat became friends with a Mouse. They found a jar of butter and hid it in a church.

The Cat could not wait to taste the butter. So, she lied to the Mouse, 'I've been invited to the church for a christening!'

Alone at the church, she ate the butter off the top of the pot. She told the Mouse that the baby was named Top-Gone.

The Cat lied twice again and ate the butter saying, 'The Babies were named Half-Gone and Full-Gone!'

During winter, the Mouse understood the Cat's trick but the Cat ate him, too.

SEPTEMBER 4

The Wolf and the Seven Young Kids

A mother Goat had seven Kids. One day, she went grazing and warned them to watch out for the Wolf.

Soon, the Wolf came and pretended to be the mother Goat. The Kids knew this and hid. But, the Wolf found the first six Kids and swallowed them.

When mother Goat returned, she was upset to only find the youngest Kid. They found the Wolf sleeping, and that the Kids were still alive in his stomach. They cut the Wolf's belly and rescued the six Kids. They put stones in his stomach that killed him when he tried to walk.

SEPTEMBER 5

The Island of Sweets

Once, a wicked Witch created an 'Island of Sweets' to trap children. She had a pet parrot that brought children to the Island.

One day, some children were playing near a forest. The parrot said, 'Do you want to go to the 'Island of Sweets?"

The children went with the parrot, but clever Sylvia hesitated. The children were trapped and made to work by the witch.

Sylvia came to rescue them. She threw a toffee at the witch's eye and took her wand to break it. The witch and her parrot were turned into stones and the children were free.

SEPTEMBER 6

The Elf's Son

Once, there lived an elf, Flash. He was the fastest messenger in the world. Everybody loved and respected him. Still, he was unhappy as he and his wife did not have any children.

Once, a gnome gave him a box to be delivered to the witch.

On his way, Flash heard a voice saying, 'Help me please!'

Flash took the box home. When he opened it, there was a baby tortoise inside. He said, 'The witch will use me for her spell if you deliver me to her.'

Flash and his wife adopted the tortoise and took care of it as their own.

SEPTEMBER 7

The Hunter and the Witch

Once, a Hunter spotted a deer in the forest and chased it on his horse. He wandered far into the dense forest. Suddenly, they reached a hut. The Deer entered it and turned into an old Witch.

Upon seeing the Hunter inside her hut, the Witch said, 'You are caught in my trap now. I shall kill and eat you.'

The terrified Hunter turned to run but the Witch caught him.

Just then, a Fairy arrived on the scene and threatened the Witch. They both cast spells at each other. At last, the Fairy won and rescued the grateful Hunter.

SEPTEMBER 8

The Kind Witch

A young Man was cutting wood in the forest. He saw an old Woman carrying a bundle of firewood and offered to help her. She agreed and gave him the bundle.

The Man placed the load on his back and walked behind her. The old Woman was in reality a Witch. She took the Man to her hut and introduced him to a young Maiden. Then, she said, 'She is the King's daughter. I saved her from a Giant. Take her back to the palace.'

The Man took the Princess back. The King married him to her as a reward.

SEPTEMBER 9

Charlie and Mary

One day, Charlie and Mary were wandering in the forest. They discovered a castle hidden behind some trees. They rushed inside and reached a large hall.

In the hall, all kinds of birds were kept in cages. Suddenly, an owl swooped down and turned into a Witch. She said, 'Welcome children. You shall be the new additions to my cage.'

However, before she could turn Charlie and Mary into birds, Charlie leapt at her and snatched her magic wand. Without it, the Witch was powerless.

Then, Charlie set all the birds free and transformed the Witch into an owl forever.

SEPTEMBER 10

The Clever Nomad

Once, a Nomad arrived in a deserted town where only a Farmer lived. He told the Nomad, 'This town is terrorized by a Dragon. He eats one person per day.'

The Nomad wasn't scared. The next day, when the Dragon came, the Nomad boldly challenged him, 'Eat me if you can but you won't be able to chew me.'

The Dragon laughed and crushed a piece of rock under its jaws to prove his strength. The Nomad picked up a stone and squeezed water out of it. Seeing his power, the terrified Dragon fled from the place and never returned.

SEPTEMBER 11

The Gnomes and the Pixies

Once, a Gnome and a Pixie fought. Their quarrel kept on growing until they declared war.

The Gnome General said to his army, 'When I raise my staff, attack. If I put it down, you must retreat back.'

The next day, as the war started, the Gnome General raised his staff to declare an attack on Pixies.

However, the smart Pixies sent their friends, a swarm of bees to attack the Gnome General.

The bees stung the Gnome General so many times that his staff fell out of his hand.

Considering it a signal, the Gnomes retreated and were defeated.

SEPTEMBER 12

The Magic Club

A young man called Yusuf worked for a magician. When he left the job, the magician rewarded him with a magical club and said, 'When you will say 'play', the club will start hitting people until you say 'stop'.

Yusuf thanked the magician and went home. When he reached, he saw that the capital city of his country was attacked by dacoits. He stood on top of a large building and yelled, 'Play.'

Hearing this, his club began to work and started hitting all the dacoits till they retreated. The King rewarded Yusuf by giving him his daughter's hand in marriage.

SEPTEMBER 13

The Battle of Darmin

Long ago, the city of Darmin was inhabited by various magical creatures.

One winter, a powerful Witch came to Darmin. Tempted by the city's beauty, she decided to rule it. Using her magical powers, the Witch became the queen. She treated all the creatures cruelly and enslaved them. A few creatures escaped and hid.

One day, a Bear came to Darmin. Learning about the Witch's cruel reign, he decided to kill her. He united all the hidden creatures and created a large army.

A fierce battle commenced. Finally, the Bear's army won and he killed the Witch. Everyone lived happily ever after.

SEPTEMBER 14

The Tin Soldier

Long ago, all toys came to life at night. In Timmy's nursery, there were many toys. At night, they all played and partied together.

One night, a Monkey came in the nursery through the window. He kidnapped the Princess Doll and jumped out.

Everyone was worried. The Tin Soldier went to her rescue. He jumped on the tree outside the window and found the Monkey.

Then, the Tin Soldier used his sword to prick the Monkey again and again till he let the Doll go. Then, he carried the Doll back to the nursery. Everyone praised his courage.

SEPTEMBER 15

The Fiery Five

Long ago, a demon came to earth. To defeat him, a sorceress assembled a team of five human beings.

These human beings were strong and courageous.

The sorceress trained them to fight the evil forces. She then gave them magical powers. After the completion of their short training, the humans united their powers. They called their team 'The Fiery Five.'

'The Fiery Five' challenged the demon to a fight. The demon unaware of their power accepted their challenge. The fight began and the demon was defeated.

Thus, the 'Fiery Five' saved earth. They thanked the Sorceress for all her help.

SEPTEMBER 16

The Ogre-Slayers

Once upon a time, two Brothers took the task of killing the Ogres. They journeyed the entire country, looking for Ogres.

One day, they were wandering in a lonely area. Suddenly, they were attacked by a bunch of Ogres.

The brave Brothers did not lose courage. They took out their guns and shot at the Ogres. Still, it had no effect on them. They retreated a little but grew more furious.

The Brothers then took out fire torches and charged at the Ogres. The Ogres fear light and were scared. The Brothers burnt them and became victorious.

SEPTEMBER 17

The Rain-God's Punishment

Once upon a time, the Rain-God became very upset with humans. He thought, 'These creatures have become very selfish and have stopped worshipping me. I shall punish them.'

Thus, the Rain- God stopped rain from falling on Earth. As the rain did not fall, the crops began to die. The humans were very upset and prayed to the Angels for help.

Sienna, the Angel of Mercy, heard their plea and came down. Seeing remorse and lament in their eyes, she convinced the Rain-God to forgive the humans.

The Rain-God agreed. He withdrew his punishment and caused the rain to fall again.

SEPTEMBER 18

The Toadstool Town

In the dense part of the forest, there was a small Toadstool town. The Forest Pixies often kidnapped the children living there. Everyone was afraid of them.

One day, a Man came to the Toadstool town. He heard of the Pixies terrorising the town. He went to the Mayor and said, 'I'll get rid of the Pixies for you but you must promise me two bags of gold coins in return.'

The Mayor agreed to the condition. Then, the Man played music on his flute. The Pixies could not tolerate the loud music. They ran from the forest and never returned.

SEPTEMBER 19

Boastful Alan

Alan liked boasting. His friends laughed and never believed him. So, to prove himself, he set out on an adventure to meet the giant in the forest.

When Alan reached the forest, suddenly, the giant leapt out from behind the trees and captured him. He made Alan his servant.

The giant said, 'Go and fetch me a jug of water.' Alan said, 'I'll get the whole stream.' Next, the giant said, 'Go and chop a log of wood.' Alan replied, 'I'll get you the whole forest?'

The giant grew scared of him and set him free. Alan's boastfulness saved him!

SEPTEMBER 20

The Elf and Fire

Long ago, the Elves didn't know how to make fire. They knew about fire but had no idea how to produce it.

One day, the Elves saw smoke rise from a nearby island.

A young Elf swam to the island to get fire. He saw some humans dancing around fire. He crept past them and took a fallen twig in his hand.

When the humans were not watching, he put fire to the twig and ran towards home. A cat noticed him and ran after him. Somehow, the Elf escaped its clutches and brought fire home.

The fire burns still!

SEPTEMBER 21

Modus' Bride

Once, an old King had three sons. To decide his heir, the King conducted a test. He called his three sons and said, 'Whoever brings me the finest crown shall become my heir.'

So, all three sons went away. The youngest son, Modus, went to a pond and met a Mermaid. She gave him a pearl-studded crown.

Seeing this, his elder brothers were jealous. They asked for another chance. This time, the King said, 'The one who has the prettiest bride shall be my heir.'

Now, Modus married the Mermaid. As she was the most beautiful, Modus became the King.

SEPTEMBER 22

The Gnome-Godmother

Once, Anna found a note under her pillow. It was an invitation from the gnomes to become the godmother of a young gnome. Anna readily agreed.

Soon, three gnomes came and took her to a cave where everything was beautifully decorated. The christening ceremony took place and Anna became the godmother of a very naughty gnome.

Now, she stayed with this gnome for many days. She taught him good manners.

The gnome king sent him to guard a big treasure to test him.

He guarded the treasure well and was praised for it. So, he thanked his godmother for training him well.

SEPTEMBER 23

The Sleep-Fairy

Ben did not believe in magic or fairies.

One night, the sleep fairy arrived and sprinkled her magic powder in Ben's eyes. Soon, Ben fell fast asleep.

After a while, he was transported to the magic land. He boarded a magic ship and sailed away.

This ship was pulled by ten swans. Mermaids and water-nymphs swam along and sang melodious songs. Colourful birds lined the horizon. There were seven rainbows in the open sky. Ben began to experience pure bliss.

Just then, Ben's alarm-clock rang and he woke up. He started believing in the magical folk from then on.

SEPTEMBER 24

The Hundred-Headed Dragon

Once, a Knight was going through a forest. Suddenly, he spotted a Dragon with a hundred heads. The Knight thought, 'I must run.'

However, as he began to run, he heard a cry, 'Help me, please!'

The Knight turned back and saw a little Girl in the clutches of the Dragon. Thus, he could not run and decided to rescue the Girl.

The Knight saw that the hundred heads of the Dragon were tied to his neck with one chord. So, he cut the chord with his sword.

Immediately, the Dragon's hundred heads fell on earth and he died.

SEPTEMBER 25

Paula and the Fairy

One evening, it snowed heavily. Paula, a poor orphan, was wandering the streets. Although it was cold, she did not dare go home as her Stepmother was very cruel.

To protect herself from the cold, Paula tried to light a matchstick but the flame died almost instantly. She lit another match but the same happened.

Unable to bear the cold, Paula lay down on the cold road. Suddenly, a gentle pair of arms lifted her up. The Fairy said, 'Don't worry child, I'm taking you home.'

The Fairy took her to heaven where Paula had to face no more hardships.

SEPTEMBER 26

The God of Fire

Long ago, during one winter, the animals of Weasely Island shivered in cold. They did every possible thing to get warmth, but all in vain.

One night, they decided to pray to the Goddess of Fire. As they were chanting the prayer, the Goddess appeared.

She said, 'You have pleased me by your devotion. Your wish shall be granted.'

The animals told the Goddess their plea. Suddenly, lightning struck the Island and set a dead tree on fire.

The animals became very happy and enjoyed the warmth as they sat near the fire. They thanked the Goddess for her mercy.

SEPTEMBER 27

The Magical Tail

Once upon a time, a Monkey was known for his magical tail in the whole forest. He used to bully everyone by extending his tail.

All the animals disliked him and kept a distance from him.

One day, a Thief came to the forest. He threatened all the animals with his gun.

The minute the Thief was about to shoot a Deer, the Monkey came in front of him. He extended his tail and caught the Thief's neck. All the animals came together and taught the Thief a lesson.

After this, the animals praised the Monkey and became his friends.

SEPTEMBER 28

The Beautiful Mermaid

Once, a beautiful mermaid lived in a sea. She was so pretty that all creatures of the sea wanted to marry her.

One day, she went in search of a handsome merman. On her way, she saw the best looking merman she had ever met.

Now, she was hesitant to talk to him because he was more beautiful than her.

So, the mermaid decided to go away. However, the merman saw her and came to her.

He said, 'You are the prettiest mermaid I have ever seen. Will you marry me?'

The mermaid readily agreed. They both married and lived happily.

SEPTEMBER 29

The Innocent Giant

Once, a hard-working Giant worked for a Villager.

One day, by mistake, the Giant dropped a golden stone into the well. So, the Villager said to the Giant, 'Go and get the stone for me.'

The innocent Giant, not knowing the depth of the well, jumped into it.

However, when he found the stone, he was not able to come out. Hearing his cries, the Villager prayed to the well Elf for help. The Elf made the water of the well rise so that the Giant could come out.

The Giant and the Villager thanked the Elf for his help.

SEPTEMBER 30

The Dwarf and the Tortoise

Once, a Dwarf guarded an underground treasure. He was very dedicated and did his work well.

One day, a Tortoise came and misled him by saying, 'You are very foolish. If I would have been in your place, I would have taken the treasure and become rich.'

Hearing this, the Dwarf thought, 'He is right. I should take this treasure.'

So, he collected all the treasure and ran away with it. On the way, the Dwarf met the Tortoise. He snatched and took away all the treasure from the Dwarf.

Now, the Dwarf realised his mistake and regretted his decision.

OCTOBER 1

The Fire Fairies

Little Ben was camping with his parents in the woods.

One night, Ben crawled out of his tent. He wanted to see the animals drinking water by the lake.

Ben reached the lake and saw a Deer family. He said, 'Wow! They look so beautiful.'

When the Deer went away, Ben decided to go back to his tent. But he forgot the way and was lost.

Soon, Ben saw some glowing lights in front of him. He followed them and reached his tent. When he looked closely, the lights were tiny Fairies.

Ben thanked the Fire Fairies and went to sleep.

OCTOBER 2

The Nightingale

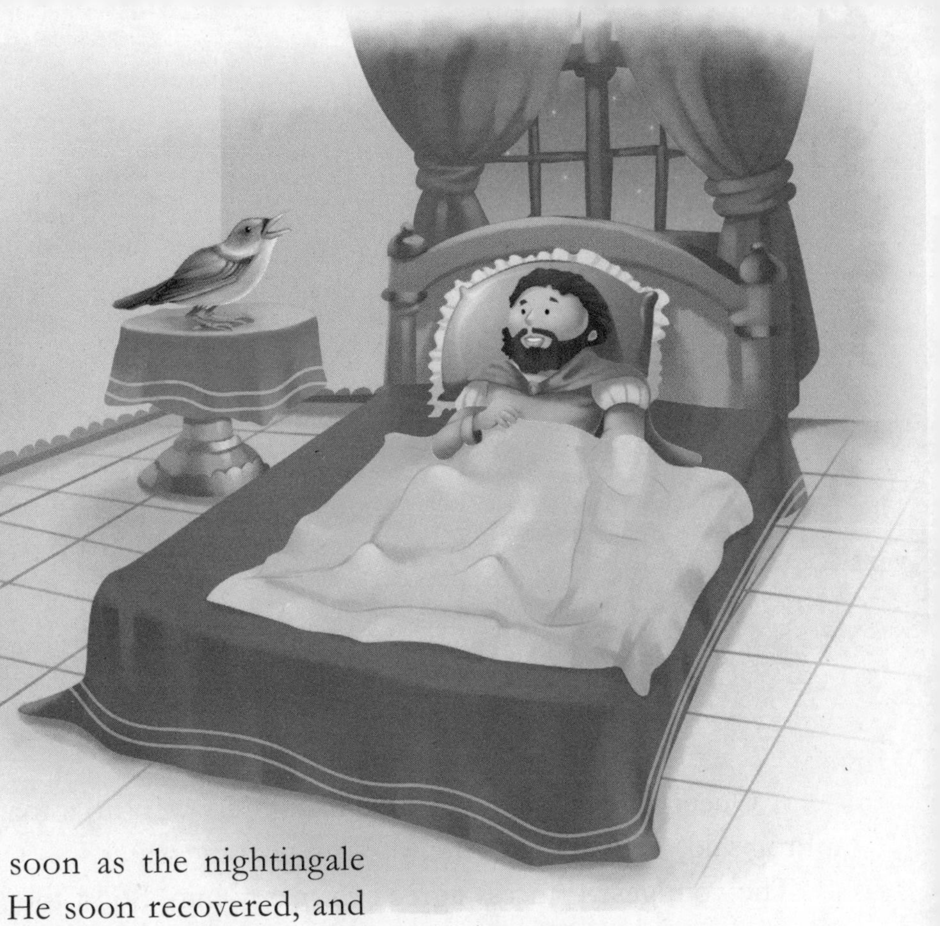

An emperor heard about the magical songs of a nightingale.

The emperor's men searched high and low, until they found a nightingale. They brought the bird to the palace.

The nightingale sang beautiful songs, which the emperor loved. He would hear its songs every day.

Then one day, the emperor was presented with a golden nightingale. He was so impressed with it, that he forgot the real nightingale. So, she flew away.

One day, the emperor fell ill. As soon as the nightingale heard this, it started singing for him. He soon recovered, and always kept the nightingale with him.

OCTOBER 3

The Brave Little Tailor

A Tailor killed seven flies in a blow and wore a belt which said, 'Seven at one blow.'

He was travelling through the country one day, when he met a Giant. The Giant thought, 'Oh, he killed seven men with a blow!'

The Giant challenged him. The clever Tailor pretended to fire an arrow, which was actually a bird. Since the 'arrow' never landed, the Giant was very scared of the Tailor's strength, and ran away.

When the King of the land heard about this, he made the clever Tailor his Chief Minister, and took good care of him!

OCTOBER 4

The Frog Prince

A Queen fell very ill. Her three Daughters went to a magical well to fetch Healing Water. There, a Frog said, 'If you marry me, you can take the water.'

The youngest Princess agreed to marry him. Soon the Queen felt better. The Frog said to the youngest Princess, 'Please give me some dinner and take me to bed.'

The Princess kept her promise, and took him to her room.

The next morning, the Frog turned into a handsome Prince! He had been cursed by a Witch, but marrying the Princess broke the curse. They lived happily ever after.

OCTOBER 5

The Swan Maiden

Once, a woodcutter saw a beautiful swan near a forest lake. He was surprised to see the swan take off its robes and emerge as a beautiful girl.

The woodcutter quickly hid the girl's swan robes so that she would not fly away.

The girl saw this and said, 'I must marry the man who steals my robes.'

The woodcutter happily married the girl. But the girl was very sad and missed being a swan.

After many years, the girl found the hidden swan robes. She immediately became a swan and flew away. She was not unhappy anymore.

OCTOBER 6

The Blessed Fairy

Once, there lived a Sea Monster in the sea. All sea creatures feared him and stayed away from him.

One day, two Mermaids were playing on a rock, when a boat came by. The Fishermen saw the Mermaids and tried to capture them. The Mermaids screamed for help.

The Sea Monster heard their cries and came there. He scared the Fishermen away and saved the Mermaids.

The Mermaids said, 'Thank you. You are very kind.'

The Sea Monster said, 'It is my duty to help all sea creatures.'

From then on, all sea creatures became the Sea Monster's friends.

OCTOBER 7

The Singing Dragon

The Magical Folk of Fairyland always heard sweet songs coming from a far-off mountain top every night. The songs put the young ones to sleep. But they never knew who sang the songs.

One day, the Magical Folk said, 'Fairy Godmother, we must find the singer and thank him.'

Fairy Godmother gave them permission to go to the mountain top. So, the Fairies, Elves, Pixies, Dwarves, and Goblins visited the mountain. They were surprised to find a Dragon playing a harp and singing. They thanked him for making the babies sleep and made him the official singer of Fairyland.

OCTOBER 8

The Lazy Frog

Once, there lived a lazy Frog who always slept and never worked. He ate from the lake and slept on water lily leaves the whole day.

One day, the Forest Fairies decided to teach him a lesson. They took the Frog with them around the forest, showing him bees collecting nectar, little birds catching worms, and ants gathering food.

Then, the Forest Fairies warned him, 'Frog, learn from these small creatures to be helpful and active. If you are seen lazing again, you will be punished.'

The Frog felt ashamed at his behaviour. He promised to never be lazy again.

OCTOBER 9

The Sea Horse Race

Once, all the sea horses in the sea held a race for their young ones. They invited the mermaid-queen to be the judge of the race.

When the race began, all the young sea horses swam towards the finish line. But a sea horse was hurt and could not complete the race. He was upset and started crying.

The mermaid-queen said, 'Don't worry, winning isn't everything. You participated in the race and that is very important.'

The young sea horse smiled and hugged her. Then, the mermaid-queen gave a special gift to the young sea horse for attempting the race.

OCTOBER 10

Naughty Keira

Little Keira was the naughtiest Fairy in the forest. One day, Keira's mother had to go for a meeting of Magical Folk. She said, 'Don't go outside the house till I return.'

But when Keira's mother left, Keira thought, 'It won't matter if I go out for a while.'

Outside, Keira saw a rainbow and flew towards it. Suddenly, a large Eagle attacked her. Keira flew as fast as possible, but the Eagle followed.

Luckily, Keira saw her mother and flew to her. Keira's mother chased the Eagle away. Keira was relieved and promised never to be naughty again.

OCTOBER 11

Samantha and the Fairies

Samantha loved to play the piano. But no matter how hard she practiced, her teacher was never happy with her. She said, 'Samantha, you need to practice more.'

Samantha finally prayed to the Fairies. That night, she dreamt that the Fairies were teaching her how to play the piano.

Next morning, Samantha played beautifully. Her teacher said, 'Samantha, you played very well today. You must perform at the piano recital on Saturday.'

Samantha performed very well at the piano recital. When the audience was clapping, she saw a group of Fairies clapping, too. She thanked the Fairies for their help.

OCTOBER 12

The Golden Bell

Once, a Pixie was gifted a golden bell by Fairy Godmother for his honesty. She said, 'When you ring the bell, it will change a person's behaviour.'

The Pixie thanked Fairy Godmother and went home. On the way, he saw two Dwarves fighting. He rang the bell and the Dwarves became friends.

When he went home, his mother scolded him, 'Where were you all this time?'

The Pixie rang the bell again. His mother said kindly, 'You must be tired, son. Go wash up and I will serve you dinner.'

The Pixie was happy and used his golden bell wisely.

OCTOBER 13

Mandrake

Once, a Princess was very ill. No one knew how to cure her. Finally, a Witch offered to make a potion. She said to the King, 'I want a Mandrake for the potion.'

The King's Minister asked, 'What is a Mandrake?'

The Witch said, 'A Mandrake is a root of a plant. You must be careful and cover your ears before you pull it out, as it lets out a high pitched wail. Its juice is the only thing that can cure the Princess.'

They searched high and low, till they found a Mandrake. Thus, they helped to cure the Princess.

OCTOBER 14

The Flower-Fairy

Once, a young Man proposed to a Girl for marriage. She replied, 'I'll marry you the day you bring me a purple rose.'

The Man searched everywhere for a purple rose but could not find one. Finally, he went to the Flower-Fairy to ask for help.

The Flower-Fairy gave him a tiny seed, saying, 'Plant this seed. In a month's time, it will grow into a purple rose.'

The Man did as the Flower-Fairy had instructed. Soon, the seed turned into a plant with a large purple rose.

The Man gave the Girl the rose and married her.

OCTOBER 15

The Naughty Pixie

Dinky was a naughty little pixie. He irritated other pixies by throwing water on them or by blowing pixie dust over them.

Soon, everyone in Pixieland was fed up of his pranks. They decided to teach him a lesson.

One day, while Dinky slept, the other pixies carried him and placed him in a Crow's nest.

A little later, when Mother-Crow woke up, she noticed the little pixie. She was annoyed and pecked Dinky hard.

Dinky shrieked aloud and fled from the nest. He realised that playing pranks was not always fun. Now, he was not so naughty.

OCTOBER 16

The Winter Festival

Long ago, Jeremy, a hunter, lived with his family on the edge of a forest.

One winter night, he saw lights twinkling and music being played in the forest.

Jeremy followed the light. Soon, he reached the middle of the forest. There, he saw all the creatures of the forest— the tree-nymphs, dwarfs, unicorns, birds and animals dancing around a huge bonfire.

The nymphs told Jeremy that it was the Winter Festival. Jeremy then drank lots of hot chocolate and ate delicious muffins.

Later, Jeremy went home and always remembered that night! He gave up hunting animals and started farming.

OCTOBER 17

The Huge Camel

A Witch lived near a village. She often troubled the villagers and asked for food. One year, there was a famine. So, the villagers could not meet the Witch's demands.

The angry Witch cursed, 'May the Earth burst open on the full moon night and a monster crush you all.'

On the full moon night, the Earth indeed split open and a huge Camel came out. Seeing him, the Witch screamed, 'Destroy this village!'

However, the Camel was sent by God. He simply lifted his foot and squashed the Witch.

The villagers were relieved at the Witch's defeat.

OCTOBER 18

The Knight and his Stallion

Once, a brave Knight wanted to buy a stallion as strong as him.

So, he went to the market. However, all the sellers said, 'Sir, we cannot sell you a suitable stallion as no one is as strong as you.'

The sad Knight went to the forest. There, he saw a white stallion tied to a tree. As he went near it, a voice came from the tree, 'I know what you need. Here is the strongest stallion in the world.'

The Knight thanked the Tree Spirit. Then, he untied the stallion and rode back to his kingdom.

OCTOBER 19

The Five-Headed Dragon

Long ago, a five-headed Dragon lived near a kingdom. Long back, the King had trapped it in a huge castle.

One day, a Prince was passing by the castle. He saw the Dragon and became curious. As he went closer, the Dragon said, 'If you untie me, I will give you a magic lamp to fulfil your desires.'

Hearing this, the foolish Prince untied the Dragon. The beast became free again and troubled the people.

The Prince was sorry for being foolish, so he begged the Fairies for help.

The good Fairies came at once and destroyed the Dragon forever!

OCTOBER 20

The Mouse-Princess

A witch cast a spell on a princess and turned her into a mouse, saying, 'The spell will be over the day my mother laughs.' The king asked all the clowns and jesters to make the witch's mother laugh but no one succeeded.

One day, the prince of a neighbouring country held a ball. Hearing this, the mouse-princess rode on a cock to the prince's palace. The witch's mother was also there. She saw the mouse-princess on a cock and burst out laughing. At once, the mouse-princess turned into a beautiful lady. Seeing her, the prince fell in love and married her.

OCTOBER 21

The Miserly Gnome

Once, there lived a foolish Gnome. He was a miser, and exchanged all his money for a bar of gold.

Then, he dug a hole in the Earth and hid the bar in it. Each day, he checked to see if his gold was safe or not.

However, one day, when he came to the spot he found that someone had stolen his gold. He could not bear the shock and cried aloud.

A Friend heard him and comforted him, 'It is bad to hoard money. It keeps coming and going.'

The Gnome took his Friend's advice and stopped hoarding money.

OCTOBER 22

The Language of Dogs

Once, a Rich Man sent his Son to study abroad. However, the Son learnt only the language of dogs. Realising this, the Rich Man threw his Son out of the house.

After wandering for a while, the Son reached a village terrorised by wild dogs. He asked the dogs, 'Why do you bark at the villagers who come here?'

The Chief Dog explained, 'An old treasure is buried here. It is our job to guard it till a young man claims it.'

Hearing this, the Son dug up the treasure. He used the money to build a shelter for dogs!

OCTOBER 23

The Girl's Song

One day, a boy and a girl were captured by a giant. He took them home and placed them in a cage.

After a while, the giant's cook came to take girl. As he picked her up, she began to sing beautifully. Her song touched the cook. He decided to set her free.

However, the girl said, 'Please let my friend also go.'

The cook could not refuse the little girl's plea and set the boy free, saying 'I will cook a large deer for the giant and he will never know.'

The two children thanked him and ran away.

OCTOBER 24

The Haunted Mill

Long ago, some Ghosts lived in an old mill. So, no one wanted to work there.

One day, a Man met the Owner for work. He promised to work in the mill despite the ghosts.

So, the Owner hired him. The Man's day at the mill was fine. However, at night, a table laden with all kinds of foods suddenly appeared. Invisible guests came and dined. The Man remained brave and joined them.

From that day on, the noises of ghosts stopped. They became friends with the Man and let the mill run peacefully during the day at his request.

OCTOBER 25

The Snow-Storm

Long ago, there was scarcity of water, and many wild animals migrated. A Hunter sat in his boat and followed them.

On the way, he was caught in a snow-storm. He was angry with the Weather God. Hearing him, the Weather God came to him and said, 'I caused the snow-storm to help you. Now, you will be able to see the footprints of animals clearly on the snow.'

The Hunter realised that he had not thought of this at all. He apologised and then easily found a deer to follow. Thus, something good came out of the snow-storm!

OCTOBER 26

Bogeyman

A bogeyman scared everyone in the forest. So, the animals decided to teach him a lesson and made a plan.

The goose hid in his water-pump, the cat curled up in his fire-place, the porcupine got under his pillow and the dog waited at his door.

When the bogeyman reached home, the dog bit him from behind the door. Next, when he lit a fire, the cat jumped and scared him.

When the bogeyman went to wash his face, the goose bit him. Finally, when he lay on his bed, the porcupine pricked him.

Scared of these animals, the bogeyman ran away forever!

OCTOBER 27

The Greedy Merchant

Long ago, a poor Carpenter and a rich Merchant went to the forest. While walking, they met a Gnome, who said, 'Fill your pockets with this coal. And see the magic!'

So, both the men filled their pockets and went home. To their surprise, the coal turned into gold on the way.

Now, the greedy Merchant wanted more. So, he went to the forest again with a large sack. He filled his sack with the gnomes' coal. However, when he returned home, the coal was still coal. Even the gold which he had got earlier had turned to coal! The Merchant cried all night for his loss.

OCTOBER 28

The Note-Book Imp

Every midnight, everything in Jake's room came to life.

Even the note-books in his school bag hopped out. The note-book imp was in-charge of them. However, one night, they ran about and played games, totally ignoring the imp. Some of them even changed their shape and height, changing from one letter to another.

Jake was fed up of rearranging all of them in the morning.

The imp felt sorry for Jake and shouted, 'You wicked creatures don't deserve to be let out. From today, nothing in this room will move at night.'

Since that day, everything remained in place in Jake's room.

OCTOBER 29

The Nymphs Awaken

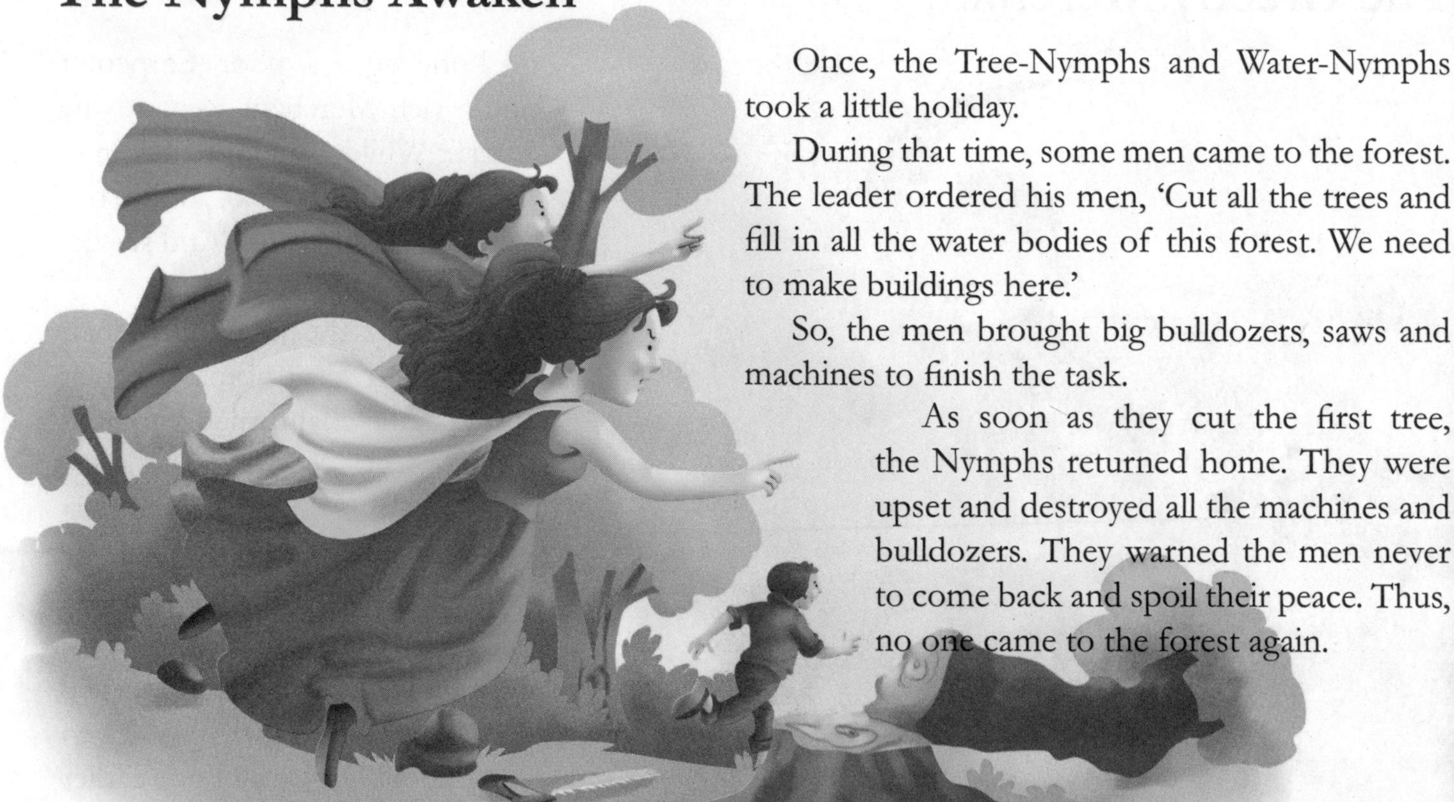

Once, the Tree-Nymphs and Water-Nymphs took a little holiday.

During that time, some men came to the forest. The leader ordered his men, 'Cut all the trees and fill in all the water bodies of this forest. We need to make buildings here.'

So, the men brought big bulldozers, saws and machines to finish the task.

As soon as they cut the first tree, the Nymphs returned home. They were upset and destroyed all the machines and bulldozers. They warned the men never to come back and spoil their peace. Thus, no one came to the forest again.

OCTOBER 30

The Wolf's Wedding

There was a young Girl who lived in the woods.

One day, she went out to look for food but couldn't find anything. A Wolf saw her and said 'May I help you?'

She agreed and took his help. Soon, she fell in love with the Wolf as he was very kind.

Finally, she went to the Forest Fairy and said 'I have fallen in love with the Wolf. Please transform me into a She-Wolf'.

The Fairy fulfilled her wish. At first, the Wolf could not recognise her but later they married each other and lived happily ever after.

OCTOBER 31

The Faithful Donkey

Once, a Man had a faithful Donkey. However, the Donkey fell ill. The Man told him, 'You have become weak. Go away!'

The poor Donkey left. On his way, he met an Elf and told him the whole story. The Elf said 'Don't worry. I will help you.'

He waved his hand over the Donkey and chanted a magical spell.

Within minutes, the Donkey became strong and young. Then, he went back to his Master and kicked him hard.

The Master was amazed at his strength and asked him to come back. However, the Donkey refused his selfish Master's offer.

NOVEMBER 1

The Snow Maiden

Mother Spring and Father Frost had no children. So, they made a Snow doll and put life into it. They named their daughter, Snow Maiden.

Snow Maiden loved to hear about humans and wished she was one.

One day, Snow Maiden met a handsome Shepherd. She was very upset because she did not know how to love. Mother Spring felt sorry for her and said, 'I will bless you with love.'

Then, Snow Maiden was able to fall in love with the Shepherd. He also loved her very much. This love warmed her heart and she finally became human.

NOVEMBER 2

The Swineherd

A prince was in love with a princess and sent her a beautiful rose that bloomed only once in a hundred years.

But the proud princess said, 'This rose will wither away. A diamond would last forever.'

The prince decided to test the princess. He dressed as a swineherd.

He made a musical pot and a rattle. The princess liked them so much that she bought them for ten kisses.

The swineherd then revealed his identity and said, 'You can kiss a swineherd but you don't appreciate the true love of a prince.'

Saying this, he returned to his kingdom. The princess regretted her pride.

NOVEMBER 3

The Sea Hare

A brave Young Man once saved the life of a magical Fox. The Fox said, 'I can help you marry the wisest and most beautiful Princess in the world.'

He told the Young Man about Princess Liz. She would only marry the man who could hide from her for three days. But no one could hide from her magic mirror, which showed the Princess everything.

The Fox, however, had a plan. He turned the Young Man into a magical Sea Hare. Now, even the Princess' mirror could not find him!

Thus, the Young Man was able to marry the Princess.

NOVEMBER 4

The Wonderful Musician

Once, a Fiddler was passing through a forest playing a tune. A Wolf, a Fox and a Hare heard his music and followed him.

The Fiddler wanted to get rid of them, so he trapped them in a net. Then, he continued his journey. On the way, the Fiddler became friendly with a Hunter.

In the meantime, the animals freed themselves and decided to attack the Fiddler. But when they came close to him, the Hunter protected his friend with his bow and arrow. The animals ran away in fear and the Fiddler thanked the Hunter for his help.

NOVEMBER 5

The Werewolf

Once, a Woodcutter was punished by a Witch for cutting trees. Because of her spell, he turned into a Werewolf on full moon nights. He then became quite fearsome and dangerous.

The Forest Fairy went to the Witch and said, 'The Woodcutter has changed his ways. Please end your spell.'

The Witch said, 'The spell can be broken only by a silver arrow.'

That night there was a full moon. The Fairy fired a silver arrow at the Werewolf. Immediately, he became a normal man once again. He was very happy and thanked both the Fairy and the Witch!

NOVEMBER 6

Bigfoot

A small group of children went trekking from their school to the mountains. They were camping in a small clearing for the night.

Benny and Bosco were the most adventurous of all the children. Benny said, 'Do you know that we might see an abominable snowman here?'

Bosco cried, 'No way! You mean the Bigfoot?'

'Yes, wouldn't that be exciting?' said Benny.

That night, the Bigfoot did visit the boys and left footprints in the snow.

Next morning, the boys were surprised! When they told the others about the footprints, no one believed them. The boys went home deciding to visit the Bigfoot the next year.

NOVEMBER 7

The Yllerion Birds

Long ago, a couple of magical birds called Yllerion lived on earth. After living for sixty years, they laid two eggs. Then, they pleaded before some birds, 'Please take care of our eggs till they hatch.'

The other birds were surprised. They said, 'Why? Where are you going?'

The Yllerion said, 'We must die to be reborn.' The other birds respected their sacrifice. So, as a mark of respect, they flew with the Yllerion birds to the sea. There, the Yllerion dived into the sea and drowned. After some months, they were reborn from the eggs they had left behind.

NOVEMBER 8

The Water Spirits

Most fishermen knew about the dangerous water spirits. They always had to avoid these spirits while fishing. Once, Richard was fishing with his grandfather. He saw a beautiful woman swimming towards him. She signalled Richard to come with her.

But his grandfather said, 'No Richard, don't look at her!' Richard asked, 'Why, grandpa?'

Grandfather said, 'These immortal water spirits can take any shape they desire. They do not drown humans but take them as slaves to serve them in their crystal palaces under the sea.'

Richard avoided looking at the woman and his grandfather quickly rowed the boat to the shore.

NOVEMBER 9

The Rare Blue Flower

Once, a Princess was poisoned and fell very ill. The King promised to reward whoever cured her.

A poor farmer named John knew how to cure her. A holy man told him, 'There is a Blue Flower on the mountain top. When the Princess smells it, she will become well. But be careful, a Dragon guards the flower.'

John climbed the mountain and saw the Blue Flower. He managed to distract the Dragon and plucked the flower.

As soon as she smelt the flower, the Princess felt better. The King thanked John and gave him a huge reward.

NOVEMBER 10

The Water Fairy

Elena went to the forest lake to fetch water every day.

One day, Elena's pot slipped and fell into the lake.

A beautiful lady appeared from the lake and said, 'I am the Water Fairy. I will bring back your pot.'

The Fairy came up with a silver pot. Elena said, 'This is not my pot.'

The Fairy returned with a golden pot. Elena cried, 'This is not my pot!'

Finally, the Fairy brought Elena's pot and said, 'I was testing you. You can keep the silver and golden pots.'

Elena thanked the Fairy, and went home happily.

NOVEMBER 11

The Song Fairy

Long ago, the Song Fairy came to Earth to teach the birds to sing. Hearing the news, the Nightingales rushed to the Song Fairy. She taught them lovely songs.

Next, the Cuckoo birds went to the Song Fairy. By this time, the Song Fairy was tired. However, she taught them to sing.

At last, the Crows went to the Song Fairy. By this time, the Song Fairy was completely exhausted. Her voice was so tired, that she could not teach them at all.

That is why the Nightingales sing beautifully, while the Crows can only caw tunelessly.

NOVEMBER 12

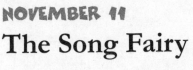

The Living Statue

In a faraway land, there was a huge statue named Colossus. A wicked Magician saw it and thought, 'Let me put life into him and make him my slave.'

So, he chanted his magical words and Colossus came to life. He was very powerful. Seeing his power, the Magician decided to defeat the King.

Mighty Colossus broke the palace gates and killed many soldiers. The King was scared and called on his bravest Knight.

The Knight was very smart. Instead of attacking Colossus, he killed the Magician. As the Magician died, Colossus froze and became lifeless again.

NOVEMBER 13

The Chimera and the Dragon

Long ago, a Lioness fell in love with a Snake. She married him and gave birth to a strange creature. This creature had the body of a lion with a snake for a tail. Everyone was scared of him, as he breathed fire. He was called 'Chimera.'

Soon, Chimera began to terrify all the animals. Seeing this, the Forest Fairy prayed to God, 'Please help us get rid of his tyrant.'

Hearing the prayers, God sent a huge Dragon to the forest. The Dragon fought a long battle with Chimera. Finally, Chimera was defeated, and all the animals were relieved!

NOVEMBER 14

Best Friends

One day, a man met a lonely giant in the forest. So, the man decided to become his friend.

Now, the man and the giant met every day. The man brought delicious cakes for the giant.

When winter came, the man's wife made woollen clothes for the giant. The giant became very fond of them.

One day, a fierce lion attacked the man. The giant saw this and saved the man. He growled so loudly that the lion ran away like a scared cat!

The man thanked the giant for saving his life. They remained best friends all their lives.

NOVEMBER 15

The Goblin and the Bird

Once, a Goblin choked on a bone while eating. A little Bird saved his life by removing the bone from his throat. However, the Goblin was quite wicked, and tried to eat the Bird!

The Bird was angry and became red in the face. She grew larger and larger, making the Goblin very scared indeed.

Then she changed into a fairy and said, 'I am the Forest Fairy. I disguised myself to see how the forest creatures treat each other. You have behaved very badly!'

The Goblin was very scared and sorry. He promised to be good in future.

NOVEMBER 16

The Pixie's Unicorn

Once, a Pixie was roaming in the woods. Suddenly, she saw a large Unicorn lying on the ground. She asked, 'What happened, friend?'

The Unicorn replied, 'I have been very ill for five days. I've tried everything but I'm still sick.'

The Pixie immediately blew some pixie-dust over him. Within seconds, the Unicorn was fit and healthy. He said, 'I'm very grateful to you, little one. How can I repay you?'

The Pixie replied, 'Please let me ride on you whenever I want to.'

The Unicorn gladly agreed. Since then, the Pixie has been riding on the Unicorn's back.

NOVEMBER 17

Pegasus

Long ago, a fairy prince had a beautiful Pegasus.

One day, he met a princess in a flower garden and became friends with her.

The princess wanted to ride the Pegasus, so the fairy prince brought it to the palace and let her ride it. Soon, the princess and the fairy prince fell in love with each other. But the king did not let them marry. He locked the princess in her room.

The fairy prince decided to rescue her. So he flew on Pegasus to the princess' window and took her away to a faraway land. They married and lived happily forever.

NOVEMBER 18

Nogisaku and the Turtle

Nogisaku was a young fisherman. Once, he saved a Turtle from some mean boys.

The grateful Turtle said, 'Come with me to the magical land of the Dragon King.'

Nogisaku agreed. They travelled together to the Dragon King's land. There, Nogisaku met the lovely Dragon Princess and fell in love with her.

But the Dragon King said, 'To marry my daughter, you will have to cross the river of fire.'

Nogisaku was worried, but the Turtle said, 'I will help you.'

Nogisaku crossed the river of fire on the Turtle's back. Thus, he was able to marry the Dragon Princess!

NOVEMBER 19

The Gnome-Family's Christmas

The gnomes celebrated Christmas with great joy. Benny, the father, sat at the dining table with his family to make the preparations. Little Timmy and his sister, Martha, went shopping and bought partridges, butter, salmon and turkey.

On their way back, some naughty imps tried to steal their groceries. But Martha bravely fought them while Timmy ran home with the groceries. Their parents praised Martha and Timmy for their bravery.

On Christmas day, their mother prepared a wonderful Christmas lunch. The family decorated the hall with lights, streamers, bells and small Christmas trees. Everyone enjoyed themselves and had a wonderful Christmas day.

NOVEMBER 20

The Wicked Sorceress

Once, a wicked Sorceress married a King. After the King's death, she ruled the kingdom very badly.

One day, she heard a Minister say, 'I wish the Queen's step-son, the Prince, would rule us.'

The Sorceress was angry. She planned to kill the Prince. But the Prince's faithful Dog heard her plan and told the Prince everything.

The next morning, the Sorceress put poison in the Prince's coffee. However, the Prince caught her red handed. She was thrown into prison, and the Prince began to rule instead. He was a good and kind ruler, and the people were very happy.

NOVEMBER 21

Ungrateful James

Once, two friends, James and Jones, were walking in the heat. They saw a huge Banyan Tree and stopped to rest in its shade.

James said, 'What a useless tree! It is so huge and lush, has such a strong trunk and branches. Still, it does not give us any fruit to eat.'

The Tree heard this. It made a branch fall on James' head. As James howled in pain, the Tree said, 'I am protecting you from the harsh sun. Still, you are ungrateful. This is why I punished you.'

James understood his mistake and apologised to the Tree.

NOVEMBER 22

The Old Woman and the Hen

One day, an Old Woman went to buy eggs. On the way, she saw a Farmer selling hens. She thought, 'If I buy a Hen instead of eggs, I can have free eggs for the rest of my life.'

So, the Old Woman bought a Hen and took it home.

The next morning, the Hen laid a golden egg. The Old Woman was delighted.

Then she got greedy and thought, 'If I feed her more food, she'll lay more eggs.'

So the Old Woman overfed the Hen and it died of indigestion! The Old Woman was sorry for her foolishness.

NOVEMBER 23

The Farmer and the Gnome

One day, a Farmer saw a Gnome sitting in his field. He thought, 'I am sure that a treasure is hidden there.'

Thinking so, the Farmer began to dig. Seeing him, the Gnome said, 'You cannot touch this treasure without my permission.'

The Farmer humbly said, 'I am very poor. I promise to take only a little of this treasure so that I can feed my children well.'

The Gnome agreed and helped him dig. As promised, the Farmer took only a few gold coins out of the huge treasure. Then, he thanked the Gnome and went home happily.

NOVEMBER 24

Mustifa's Wish

Long ago, there lived a poor man named Mustifa. Every day, he prayed to Erebus, the God of wealth.

One day, Erebus went to Mustifa's home as a Beggar and said, 'I am very hungry. Please give me some food.'

Mustifa gave all the food that he had to the beggar. Seeing this, Erebus revealed his true identity and said, 'Ask for anything that you want.'

Mustifa replied, 'I want to turn whatever I wish into gold.'

Erebus granted Mustifa his wish and left. Mustifa used his boon very wisely all his life and helped all the poor and needy.

NOVEMBER 25

A Poor Man in Heaven

One day, a Poor and a Rich Man went to Heaven. As the Rich Man went inside, the Poor Man heard trumpets blown.

The Poor Man also went inside. But now, there were no trumpets blown. He was disappointed and asked, 'Are rich people preferred over poor ones even in Heaven?'

The Angels replied, 'Everyone is treated equally here. It's just that poor people arrive here every day. We rarely get to see a rich person come to heaven instead of hell.'

Now, the Poor Man understood the plight of rich men after death. He did not feel upset anymore.

NOVEMBER 26

Corin and the Giant

One day, young Corin went to the forest alone. There, he saw a huge house. A huge Giant and his Wife lived here.

As Corin went near the house, he heard a voice, 'I smell a boy. He will serve as a good meal for us. Yummmmm!'

Hearing this, Corin began to run away. However, the Giant ran behind him and caught him. Corin cried for help.

Suddenly, a huge Bird swooped over the Giant. It was so large that the Giant was terrified. He dropped Corin and ran away.

Corin thanked the Bird. He never wandered about alone again!

NOVEMBER 27

Good Manners

Once, an ill mannered Boy lived in a village. He troubled cats and dogs, threw water on people, and stones at innocent birds.

One day, an Elf saw this Boy and decided to teach him good manners. He carried the Boy to Elf Land and said, 'You can go back only once you learn to say 'Sorry', 'Please' and 'Thank You'. You must stop troubling others. You must be disciplined and learn table manners.'

The Boy was scared, and agreed. Over the days, his behaviour became much better.

Finally, the Elf sent him home when he became a perfect gentleman.

NOVEMBER 28

The Nymph's Veil

Long ago, a farmer lived near a forest. He knew a lot about the magical creatures.

One day, he was walking through the forest, when he saw something. He went closer and saw a sparkling veil hanging on a branch.

He took the veil and went home.

That night, a beautiful maiden appeared in his bedroom. She said, 'I am a nymph. Please return my veil.'

The farmer said, 'How do I know that you are speaking the truth?'

The nymph began to dance in the air. The farmer knew that only nymphs could dance so beautifully. So, he returned the veil.

NOVEMBER 29

The Satyr and the Witch

One day, a Satyr was crossing the forest. He lost his way and reached a Witch's cottage. She saw him and commanded, 'Come, dine with me.'

The Satyr was terrified. He knew that the Witch would try to eat him for dinner.

The Witch placed a large pot of water on the fire. Then, she chopped vegetables and put them in the pot.

Seeing this, the Satyr had an idea. He pushed the Witch from behind and made her fall in the boiling pot.

Before she could rub the water out of her eyes, the Satyr ran off to safety!

NOVEMBER 30

The Bluebird's Faith

There once lived a Bluebird who wished to have blue feathers as sadly she had dull, grey feathers.

A Pixie told her, 'If you dive in the magical pond daily, your feathers will turn blue.'

So, the Bluebird began to dive in the pond daily. However, instead of turning blue, her feathers started falling off. Still, she didn't lose faith and dived every day.

Seeing this, the Water Nymph was pleased. She made the Bluebird's feather grow back in beautiful shades of blue. Seeing them, the Bluebird was delighted. She thanked the Pixie and the Water Nymph again and again!

The Golden Goose

Once, a young Man was kind to a Dwarf in the forest. The Dwarf said, 'I will give you a Golden Goose in return for your kindness.'

When the Man was returning home, many people noticed the Golden Goose. They tried to grab the Goose but they got stuck to it magically.

A Princess saw this and laughed heartily. The King was overjoyed as his daughter had not laughed in years. He put the Man through many tests before marrying his daughter to him. The Man succeeded in the tests with the help of the Dwarf and married the Princess.

DECEMBER 2

The Three Feathers

A King wanted an heir to his throne. So he said to his three sons, 'Bring the most expensive carpet, a finest ring and the most beautiful woman in the world.'

Then, he blew three feathers into the air to decide the direction his each son should take.

The first two brothers could not find the desired possessions.

The youngest son met a Frog and befriended it. It brought him the most expensive carpet and the finest ring. Then, it turned itself into the most beautiful Woman ever seen and married him.

The youngest son became the king's heir.

DECEMBER 3

The Three Sons of Fortune

A dying father said, 'Sons, a Rooster, a Scythe and a Cat are simple things but they will bring you great fortune when you sell them in a land where they are unheard of.'

After their father's death, the first son went to a land where no one knew how to see time. So, the people bought the Rooster from him for a lot of money.

The second son sold the Scythe to the people who did not know how to harvest their grains.

The third son sold his Cat to people who were troubled by mice.

Thus, they all became rich.

DECEMBER 4

The Three Little Birds

Once, a king married a maiden. The king's two ministers married the maiden's sisters.

The queen gave birth to two boys and a girl, but her jealous sisters threw them in the river. A fisherman saved them.

The angry king imprisoned the queen for losing his children.

Each time a baby was thrown, a little bird came to live in the palace.

One day, the birds spoke, 'Your children were thrown into the river by the queen's sisters. A fisherman took them home.'

The king found his children and apologised to the queen. Her sisters were severely punished.

DECEMBER 5

The Kind hearted Witch

Once, an old witch lived in a cottage outside the village near the hill. One day, a heavy storm hit the hills and big boulders started to roll down the hill. The villagers got terrified, packed their valuables and ran outside the village. They asked the witch to come with them.

The witch asked the villagers not to panic. She instantly lit a big fire and placed a pot of water to boil. Along with, she started chanting the magical words and sprinkled magic powder in the boiling water. A big white bubble rose from the pot, and enveloped the entire village.

Boulders rolled down the hill but the bubble saved the villagers and their houses.

DECEMBER 6

The Tooth Fairy

A boy named Jessie never believed in Fairies. He said to his friends, 'But why can't I see them? They just don't exist.'

That night, Jessie lost a tooth. Before throwing it away, he thought, 'Let me check if the Tooth Fairy really takes my tooth at night.'

He hid his tooth under the pillow and pretended to sleep.

In the middle of the night, Jessie heard a noise under his pillow. He lifted it up and saw a colourful Tooth Fairy. He was shocked but the Fairy blessed him with her wand.

Jessie promised never to disbelieve in Fairies.

DECEMBER 7

The Lovable Bear

A family of three Bears, a mother, father and a lovable daughter lived up on a mountain. They always waited under an apple tree as the magical apple tree dropped hundreds of apples.

They would exchange the apples for honey from the bees and lived a peaceful life.

One day, the apple tree decided to be selfish and stopped dropping apples. The lovable daughter Bear said, 'Papa, please help me climb on your back and I will pluck the apples.'

The apple tree apologised to the Bears for being selfish and gave a big hug to the lovable daughter Bear.

DECEMBER 8

Elf and the Greedy Woodcutter

One day, a woodcutter named Peter found a cave full of treasure in the forest. Just as he was looking at the treasure, Norvin, the Elf, entered the cave. Norvin asked, 'What are you doing inside my cave? Peter replied that he had found the cave and wants half the gold. Norvin gave Peter two bags of gold.

But Peter was a greedy man. He decided to steal more gold at night. When he reached the cave he found that everything had turned to coal. Norvin knew that Peter would come back. So, he had put a spell and made gold look like coal to Peter. Suddenly, Peter's ear started to grow big.

Peter promised never to try to steal again. Norvin removed the spell and Peter ran all the way home!

DECEMBER 9

The Baby Pegasus

Once, a Baby Pegasus wanted to fly. But his mother said, 'It is too early for you to fly, my dear. When you will turn fourteen years of age, you will magically fly.'

Still, he would not listen.

One day, when the Pegasus' mother was away, he thought, 'I will show Mother that I can fly too.'

He became over confident to prove that his mother was wrong that he tried to fly off a cliff. Soon, he found himself falling.

Just then, two Angels came and rescued him. The Baby Pegasus promised that he will always listen to his mother.

DECEMBER 10

The Magical Lake

There was a magical lake with powers to turn whoever bathed in it into mermaids.

One day, a group of unicorns wanted to play in the lake's water. The minute, they stepped into the water, they turned into mermaids.

The unicorns enjoyed being mermaids for some time. Then, they were fed up as they could not walk or fly. They pleaded with the magical lake, 'Please help us turn back.'

The Lake said, 'Use your power of mind and you will change.'

When the unicorns willed with confidence and they finally turned. They happily ran on the land and finally flew away.

DECEMBER 11

Fairy and the Dragon

One night, Fairy Riri was fast asleep. She woke up, hearing someone shouting for help, but she could not see anyone.

The next morning, she stood in front of the little fishpond and created the magic spell. The water of the pond became a mirror. She saw a handsome Prince trapped inside a cottage in the woods, guarded by a dangerous dragon, in it.

Riri flew to the cottage and hid behind a tree. When the dragon was asleep she tied him with magic chains. Then, she freed the Prince. Then they both quickly escaped from the cottage.

The Prince fell in love with beautiful Riri and asked her to marry him. Riri liked the kind Prince very much. They both returned to the Prince's palace and got married.

DECEMBER 12

The Helpful Fred

Once, three brothers, Ed, Eddie and Fred met an old man in the forest. He asked them to help him carry logs to his cottage.

Lazy Ed refused to help. Greedy Eddie asked for ten gold coins. But, Fred carried the logs to his cottage.

The old man said, 'I am a wizard. If ever you need help, just think of me.'

One day, the brothers' cottage caught fire. Ed and Eddie were trapped. Fred immediately thought of the old man.

Just then, the wizard appeared and saved them. They thanked the wizard and were never greedy or lazy again.

DECEMBER 13

The little Sapling

Once, a Gardener planted a little Sapling near a big mango tree. He gave equal care to all his plants, but the Sapling refused to grow.

The worried Gardener called the Garden Fairy for help. At first, the Sapling did not talk. But the Sapling finally said, 'I am scared to grow in front of this huge and brave mango tree. I feel ashamed of my little branches and leaves.'

The Fairy smiled and said, 'Why should you be ashamed of yourself when we all are so unique?'

The Sapling had never thought of that! It finally started growing and turned into a beautiful young peach tree.

When the Garden Fairy visited next, the tree thanked her for her advice by giving her peaches from its branches!

DECEMBER 14

The Fairy Princess' Friend

Once, the King of Fairyland was very sick. Only the magical herbs could save him. Since a fierce Giant guarded the herbs, everyone was scared of going there. So, the Fairy Princess disguised herself as a young boy and set out all alone.

On her way, the Princess met a young man named Frederick. When Fredrick learnt of the Fairy Princess' plan, he said, 'It is not safe to go to the forest alone. I'll accompany you.'

Fredrick and the Princess reached the forest late at night. When Fredrick was asleep, she went looking for the herb. The Giant was guarding the herbs. The Princess became invisible and took some magic herb.

The next morning, she told Fredrick, 'I have got the herbs. Now we can go back home.' Fredrick was surprised when he realised that the boy was actually Fairy Princess!

She thanked him and they became friends for life.

DECEMBER 15

The Enchanted Spring

A prince and his minister went riding in a forest. The minister wanted to be the king and wanted to trap the prince. So, he said, 'I have heard of an enchanted spring. Let's taste its magical waters.'

The prince drank the water and suddenly turned into an old man. The minister ran away slyly. Then, a giant appeared and said, 'I am the keeper of this forest. The fairy-queen will help you.'

The fairy-queen gave the prince the nectar of a magical flower, which turned him to his true self.

The prince thanked her and returned to his kingdom.

DECEMBER 16

The Golden Bird's Egg

Once, there lived two naughty Pixies named Cubby and Bobby. They caused troubled to everyone in Fairyland.

One day, a pair of Golden Birds cried, 'Help us, Fairy God Mother! We cannot find our egg.'

Fairy God Mother sent her Unicorn, Thandy, who was good in finding missing things. Thandy went to the Bird's nest and looked for clues. He found a small glove. Then, he found Cubby and Bobby sitting around a fire in the woods.

Thandy noticed a missing glove on Bobby's hand. Fairy Godmother punished the Pixies for stealing the egg and Thandy was rewarded.

DECEMBER 17

The Cat Princess

A King had three sons. One day, he said, 'I will give my kingdom to whoever brings me the finest Horse.' The Youngest Prince met a Cat who said, 'If you serve me for seven years, I will give you a fine Horse.'

The Prince chopped wood and built her a cottage.

When the Prince returned back, his brothers teased him for being foolish.

But one day, a beautiful Princess came with a fine Horse. She said, 'Prince, I am the Cat that you worked for. A witch had cast a spell on me.'

She married the Prince and lived happily.

DECEMBER 18

The Dove and the Girl

Once, a girl ran away to the forest as her wicked stepmother troubled her a lot. There, she met a magical dove, who gave her a key and said, 'Unlock that tree. You will find food and a bed to sleep on.'

Next day, the dove requested, 'Now please help me. Go to the witch's house. Do not speak to her but bring a ring from there.'

The girl helped the dove. Then, he wore the ring and turned into a prince. The witch had cast a spell on him and his kingdom. He married the girl and lived happily.

DECEMBER 19

The Impressive Performance

Once, an Old Pixie called his three sons and said, 'I want to give my house to whoever learns and spends his life well.'

The first son became a barber and shaved a running rabbit. The second son became a blacksmith. He put horseshoes on the horses while they were drawing a carriage at full speed.

The third son became a fencing master. He stood in the rain and did not get wet because he moved his sword swiftly to stop raindrops. The Old Pixie gave him the house. But that son shared it with his brothers and lived happily.

DECEMBER 20

The Prince's Secret Friends

Once, a Queen beheaded every Suitor who came to marry the Princess if he failed to complete the tasks she asked him to do.

A Prince was in love with the Princess and went to compete in the Queen's tasks with his secret friends.

When the Queen gave ten plates of food to eat, the Prince's fat friend completed the task. When he was asked to find lost items, the Prince's friend who had sharp eyes completed the task. Thus, the Prince emerged a clear winner.

The Queen was forced to give up and marry her daughter to the Prince.

DECEMBER 21

The Lamb and the Fish

Once a witch Stepmother cast a spell on her Stepchildren and turned them into a Lamb and a Fish. Then, she said to her cook, 'We will have guests tonight. So, cook the Lamb.'

Before the cook took the Lamb out of the pen, the Lamb spoke to the Fish, 'Good bye, Sister!'

The cook grew suspicious when the Lamb and the Fish bid farewell to each other.

So, she took them to a Wise Magician. He knew that they were the two Stepchildren. He turned them into children and sent them far away from their wicked Stepmother.

DECEMBER 22

The Donkey Prince

Once, a King and Queen went to a Witch as they wanted a child.

The Witch gave them a potion to drink. Soon, they were blessed with a Donkey as a child.

The Donkey grew up to be wise and skilled Prince. He went to the neighbouring kingdom and won a challenge. He was married to the Princess there.

The Princess noticed that the Donkey Prince took off his skin at night and became a handsome man. She said to her father, 'Hide his skin.'

The King hid the Donkey skin and the Prince never changed into a Donkey again.

DECEMBER 23

The Troublesome Dwarfs

Reid was upset. Something or the other was always going wrong. His socks were missing or his shoes were in the wrong place or the cookie jar was empty.

Reid decided to catch the trouble makers. That night Reid kept awake and saw five thumb-sized Dwarfs come through the window. They spoilt his work and threw his toys around.

The next day, Reid hung five socks under the window. At nightfall, the Dwarfs jumped right into the socks trap!

Reid quickly closed the mouth of all the socks and asked, 'Who are you?' They replied, 'We are Dwarfs. We enjoy troubling children, but we promise never to trouble anyone again. Please release us, for if we are found in a house at daybreak we will die.'

Reid set them free. The naughty Dwarfs never troubled children again!

DECEMBER 24

Tiny Tubby

Tubby was very small, but brave. His father was a tall, brave warrior and his mother was the Dwarf Queen.

Everyone in the village loved Tubby but no one wanted to marry him because he was small. This made Tubby very sad.

One day, Tubby saw eagles crowding around banyan tree. A pretty girl as small as him was trying to save herself from the Eagles. Tubby quickly pulled out his sword and chased the Eagles away.

The girl was none other than the Princess of Tiny-land! She thanked Tubby and said, 'I feel very scared among all the tall people! Everyone in my kingdom is small.' Tubby took her back to her kingdom. They got married and lived happily together.

DECEMBER 25

The Magical Garden

A King had a beautiful Daughter who fell sick one day. The Royal Doctor said, 'She will be healed only if she ate apples from a Dwarf's magical garden.'

The King announced, 'Whoever brings the apples for my daughter will marry her!'

The Dwarf was a wicked man and he cast spell on anyone who came close to his garden. But a peasant's son bravely went to the magical garden and plucked some apples.

When the Dwarf caught him, he told him the truth. The Dwarf was impressed with his honesty and let him go. He married the Princess and lived happily.

The Dragon's Horns

Once, a Dragon kidnapped a Princess and kept her in a tower. The King was very upset but his Knight said, 'Don't worry, my lord! I will bring the Princess back.'

Then, he went in search of the Princess. On his way, he met the Dragon's mother who said, 'My son is ferocious. If you don't want to provoke him, pull out his horns while he is sleeping. In this way, you can defeat him easily, too.'

The Knight thanked the kind woman and pulled out the Dragon's horns. Then, he fought him and brought the Princess back safely.

DECEMBER 27

The Animal Languages

Once, a Young Man spent many years learning the languages of Dogs, Birds and Frogs. His father thought him to be very foolish and sent him away to the forest.

There, he rescued a Rich Man's beautiful daughter from a frightening Giant by talking to Frogs and Birds.

The Rich Man was impressed and said, 'You saved my daughter's life. I give my daughter's hand in marriage to you and make you my heir.'

The Young Man married the beautiful girl and lived happily with all the riches he earned because of the three animal languages he had learnt.

DECEMBER 28

Hope – The Careless Fairy

The fairy Hope was powerful but careless. The Fairy-Queen wanted Hope to use her powers wisely. One day, the Fairy-Queen asked Hope to help poor and hungry children.

When Hope visited the children, she discovered that her wand wasn't there. She had lost it. Suddenly, it started raining. Hope saw the poor children shivering but she could not help. The Fairy-Queen appeared and said to Hope, 'You are kind and want to help everyone, but you are very careless. I found your wand in the forest. Take it and help the children.' From that day onwards, Hope became careful.

DECEMBER 29

The Tooth Fairy's Sweet

One morning, Sean woke up and found that he had a loose tooth. He cried aloud for his Mother. She cuddled him and said that it's time for the Tooth Fairy to come. 'Who is that, Mother?' asked Sean.

His Mother explained, 'When babies grow, Tooth Fairy takes their baby teeth and gives them a set of brand new teeth.' But Sean was scared of the pain.

That night, Tooth Fairy came in his dream and said, 'Each time you have a loose tooth, I'll leave this magic sweet under your pillow. Eat it and you will lose your tooth without pain.'

Sean awoke and found the magic sweet under his pillow. And, the Tooth Fairy quietly took his loose tooth at night.

DECEMBER 30

Two Golden Birds

Once upon a time, a boy called Sam lived in a village. Sam's parents had died when he was very young. He lived with his Uncle who treated him badly.

One night, Sam sneaked out of the window and ran into the Forest. But the Forest was a scary place. Poor Sam called out to his Mother for help.

Suddenly, two Golden Birds appeared and asked Sam to follow them. Sam was scared but he decided to follow the Birds. He reached a small hut in the middle of the forest. There lived a kind and loving couple who longed for a child.

The Birds were Angels in disguise. The couple wanted a child and Sam needed a loving family, the Angels helped them find each other.

DECEMBER 31

The Dwarf and the Giants

Once, a cunning Dwarf persuaded a man to give up his only son in return of a treasure. But when the Dwarf came for the boy, the Man realised his mistake and refused to give his son.

Then, the Dwarf said, 'I'm ready to give up your son if you bring a pair of magical boots from a group of Giants.'

The Man agreed and went to the Giants. They asked him many riddles which he answered correctly. After taking the magical Boots and the gifts from the Giants, the Man returned to the Dwarf who left his son unharmed.